WOLF IN A
BEAVER COAT

WOLF IN A
BEAVER COAT

a novel by

Rosario Lloret

TIGHTROPE BOOKS

Tightrope Books
167 Browning Trail
Barrie, Ontario. L4N 5E7
www.tightropebooks.com

Editor: Halli Villegas and Sèphera Girón
Copy editor: Sèphera Girón
Cover and typography: Dawn Kresan
Author photo credit: Martin Vegt

Printed and bound in Canada

We thank the Canada Council for the Arts, the Ontario Arts
Council, and the Government of Ontario through the book publishing tax credit for their support of our publishing program.

Library and Archives Canada Cataloguing in Publication

Lloret, Rosario, author
  Wolf in a beaver coat / Rosario Lloret.

ISBN 978-1-926639-71-0 (PBK.)

  I. TITLE.

PS8623.L67W64 2013   C813'.6   C2013-905701-3

To my mother, who opened my eyes to Life and to Magic.

This story was born after living six years in the aboriginal communities of the Northwest Territories in the Canadian Arctic, especially in the Dogrib Nation: thirty-nine thousand square kilometers of wilderness between Great Bear Lake and Great Slave Lake. The Canadian Government returned this land to the Dogrib First Nations in 2005 in a belated attempt for historical justice.

This is a novel marked by the uncertainty and the surprise of an environment able to annihilate you in a few minutes if you ignore its stern laws. Conversely, this same environment generously offers the fresh breath of its unpolluted pure blue sky, the pungent intensity of life in the taiga, the marvel of the bluish snow in the long Arctic night beneath the liquid light of the Northern Lights and the revealing and serene presence of the aboriginals with their scent of hickory smoke and tanned hide, their stories loaded with hardship and magic.

The elder Dogrib hunters, mourning with quiet acceptance the collapse of their culture and their values at the hands of the incomprehensible White Man and his industry have been, jointly with my own ghosts and dreams, the main inspiration for this novel. It is composed mainly of stories I have heard from them, others I have witnessed and others that were and never should have been. All these stories have progressively grown and intertwined like vine, pushing and caressing one another, changing and evolving like smoke in a teepee.

I

The snowmobile shook slightly. Hardly a hesitation, more like the concealed cough of a white man. An insignificant oscillation in the performance of the engine that might have gone unnoticed by anybody else. But a Dogrib knows his machines the same way he knows the animals he hunts, as living beings, full of threat and potential. So Amorak knew immediately that the shake would soon repeat, perhaps, with a little bit of luck, only a couple of times. Then the engine would die. He didn't even contemplate stopping and having a look because he didn't have the necessary tools, and with the thermometer on the dashboard flashing at fifty below, he couldn't take off his helmet or his mittens to work.

In front of him, on the narrow ice track cut deep in the taiga, the wind raised snow dust anacondas in the light of his machine's powerful headlights. These were the first warnings of the imminent whiteout that in spite of his thick snowsuit and his heavy snowmobile boots, at this temperature, could kill him in less than an hour.

He was somewhere on the subarctic ice road that linked the small population of Rae-Edzo, to Nogha Ti and Rae Lakes. An ice road usable for only a couple of months every year, during the coldest part of winter, by consolidation of ice over the many rivers and lakes, which allowed heavy trucks to supply fuel and other necessary goods to small communities. There was no village, house, or inhabited place in the more than one hundred kilometers that separated him from Nogha Ti, nor signal for his cell phone.

"Shit!" he shouted, in an attempt to replace fear with rage, but his voice resounded inside his helmet, returning a tone of anguish and desolation that made his fear even more raw.

He had already felt that malfunction of the engine before, but he had been postponing leaving the snowmobile in the workshop, as it had never been convenient for him to go without it for the minimum one week that the dealership demanded to repair the engine, plus the possible added delay due to the wait for spare parts. His wife had been warning him for weeks and, should she have been with him now, would most surely have used this anguishing occasion to say a triumphant "I told you so!" before dying from hypothermia. But she wasn't here. Amorak was alone now, in the worst of times and places, a few minutes from a snowstorm, far away from any refuge and unable to foresee how much more his snowmobile could take. Hell, it was an impressive thousand engine and 177 horses bitch. According to advertising and logic, it couldn't fail. It shouldn't fail.

The intense cold had already permeated through his clothing, and once the blizzard started to blow big time, the temperature would drop even more, probably to less than sixty below with the wind chill factor. The only cargo he had on the tattered sled were bootleg whisky bottles for Nogha Ti, his home community, where the alcohol prohibition by-laws made booze trafficking a very profitable business. And when one was a bootlegger, one couldn't afford to carry a survival kit, or a blanket, or an axe in the sled or the small storage compartment. One had to optimize space. In order to make the journey and the risk worth taking, one had to stuff every nook with bottles and mickies and trust in the prodigious and precarious balance that allowed someone like him to survive in the merciless environment—at least until now. A bootlegger had to use alternative routes inaccessible to the heavy RCMP Land Rovers to get to Nogha Ti. He followed routes carved in the taiga by the dog sleds of his ancestors, forming an arcane network which could lead to death if you misread it, or entered it carelessly. You had to sell the whisky discreetly. Most of it he and his friends drank. And of course, his wife. She was the big dark hole in his life that seemed incapable of happiness or laughter. The mere thought of her always made him feel gloomy and guilty.

Now all his senses were focused on tracking the performance of the engine. If he was lucky, perhaps he could get to the refuge that lay midway between Rae-Edzo and Nogha Ti before visibility was nil. Before the machine stopped completely. The mere thought of that made the nape of his neck tingle with apprehension and his throat feel dry with fear. His eyes, like an eagle's, were fixed on the left side of the way, where the refuge should be.

The refuge was a bare log cabin that had been built on the border of the road to shelter trappers, hunters or just travelers like him, experiencing a breakdown or assaulted by the maddened climate of the region. Its roof supported a twenty foot metal post on which a red light blinked permanently, making a funny clack sound that could be heard at about a hundred meters.

He had never been inside. Sometimes, while passing by, he had seen people stopping there. Mainly old-timers. Small groups often gathered there to rest a little, light a fire, make some tea and shake the chill off the "ol' bones" while exchanging tall hunting tales. He supposed there had to be some bunk beds there, a table and a couple of chairs, a cupboard with some cans of food, tea and coffee and a fire stove. And although he had never had the curiosity or the wish to enter the refuge before, in that moment there was not a place in the world that seemed more desirable to him.

Without a GPS, Amorak had no possible way to know what point of the track he was on. That was another chant his wife had been exhaustively repeating: that he should install a GPS in the snowmobile. His answer had always been that he did not need a machine to know where he was, that GPS was for whites and idiots. Now, to be fair, it would have been wonderful to have a GPS to know what distance he was from the refuge, because in the darkness and with the scarce visibility, it was impossible to distinguish the small foothills and landmarks that normally made the way recognizable, even familiar. *It can't be too far*, he said to himself, striving to actually believe it, to fight off despair. Soon he would see the red light that blinked on top of the high post over the roof of the cabin, a lighthouse in the arctic night. The red beacon that made that funny click as it blinked, "paff, paff, paff." He summoned the exact hue of the sharp red light, the precise sound of that saving click, the smell of smoke when someone was making tea.

Hell, there it was again. The jerk of the engine, this time more brusque. This time even a white man would have noticed it. He clenched his teeth, the black sparks of his eyes uneasily watching the left side of the track, where, in any moment, the red light would show like a salvation star, like the one in Bethlehem: "paff, paff, paff."

The headlights cast their insufficient light on a horizontal snow-fall that the wind thrust at him like a frenzied swarm. It would soon become a wall impenetrable by light. Would he see the red light then? Would he hear its faint click through the noise of the engine and the howling of the wind, through the tight capsule of his helmet? Suddenly, the chilling realization came to his mind that he might have already passed the refuge. Visibility was very poor. It was perfectly possible to have overlooked the red light. Fear squirmed in his stomach.

He was panting now, and this was bad. He knew panic suppressed reaction capacity and left a man at the mercy of circumstances, and the circumstances could not be worse. He tried to calm down by taking deep breaths. "Remember, you are a Dogrib, brought up to face the toughest conditions in the Planet. Your father taught you how to survive a whiteout, remember?"

The memory of that training remained in a dusty corner of his brain, the corner where he stored all the traditional wisdom to make room for money-making skills. The tanned serene face of his father looked at him now from that dusty corner, with serious concern. His real father, that was. The second one. The one who had chosen him as a son, not the first one, who had been hardly an incandescent nightmare that he now kept, not effortlessly, away from his memory most of the time.

"Do not lose your calm," his father—the good one—had said. "Remember that predators always choose the prey that lose their calm, and why is that?"

"Because fear makes them weak?" Amorak had answered.

"That's correct. And the snowstorm is the worst of all predators. Do not waste your heat," he had told him as he turned the hourglass his mom used to measure time for boiled eggs.

"Look at the sand," he pointed at the upper part of the hourglass. "In a snowstorm, your heat is like this sand: it slowly but consistently slips away from you, and once it is all gone, you're dead." Both, father and son had stared hypnotized at the sand softly slipping through the slim waist of the hourglass. Now, what else had the old man said? "Look for refuge in the bush." What else was there? There was much more to it, of course, but right now he could not bring it back to his mind, because right now panic was taking over.

Should he stop the snowmobile and make himself a small refuge in the bush? But, how? He did not have an axe to cut the branches or anything to help him light a fire. How long could he survive? Were his winter clothes going to protect him against this lethal cold? He looked at his shaking hands on the handlebars, wrapped in moose hide mitts with fox lining that his mother had made for him, beaded with green and red flowers. He held on tighter to suppress the shaking.

He strove to focus on tracing back his journey. He had passed the detour for the abandoned Colomac mines, but he could not say how long ago, even though his survival depended on remembering. The more he turned over the thought in his mind, the more elusive the answer became. The blue screen on the dashboard indicated it was 8:45 p.m. but this information was irrelevant as he could not even remember what time he had left Yellowknife. The last place he had visited had been, of course, the liquor store, where he had purchased the bottles to bootleg. Before that, he had a couple of drinks in McKenzie Lounge with his friend, Lou Molakoe.

Lou was almost always in the MacKenzie Lounge. One could almost always count on his presence if one decided to have a drink there. It was not necessary to call him, since he was there, as if by tacit agreement he had the obligation to attend the bar day after day, like a clerk in his office. Some years ago, Molakoe had worked with him in the Akati diamond mine, three hundred kilometers northwest from Yellowknife, where the company flew its workers to work in two-week turns, twelve hours a day, and then flew them back to take one week rest. The place was a giant well surrounded by processing premises, conveyors, and heavy machinery. From the air, it looked like a crater in the middle of nowhere, only snow and emptiness around it. And diamonds, for sure: for whoever could buy them. Workers did not even get to see them. Machines like dinosaurs extracted rocks from the pit, colder than death itself. The material passed through a closed conveyor where laser light located the diamonds and then compressed air shot to separate them from the rock and make them fall into another conveyor, where, under the strictest of scrutiny, other workers extracted the valuable stones. Molakoe's job had consisted of washing the protective work overalls, and to eliminate, through a complicated procedure, any trace of the lethal chemical substances to which workers were exposed in the mine. From his experience in those mines, he had contracted a chronic cough of unknown nature that alcohol and tobacco made worse every day. He had also acquired sheer bitterness from helplessly witnessing the darkest side of human iniquity.

Amorak's job, on the other hand, had led him every day to the deepest part of the pit, onboard a bulldozer with wheels as high as a two-story house. There he spent twelve hours digging under the light of the machine's headlights, lights that kept him dazzled as a deer on the road but could not banish the tomb-like feeling of the place. When, after his twelve-hour shift, he came out of there, blinded and frozen, he always had a couple of clandestine drinks with his friend Lou. Just a couple, though. He had to stay in control, since alcohol was severely prohibited in the worksite and in the workers' camp. The punishment for breaking this law was outright dismissal without the possibility of being re-hired, which ultimately happened to Lou.

With time, they became friends. Not best friends, as in Butch Cassidy and the Sundance Kid, but they felt comfortable together. There was no need to talk much, no need of confrontations or fabrications to hide the truth that both liked to drink and neither of them liked to drink alone. That was the basis for their friendship. When Lou was finally let go by the Company because of his addiction to alcohol, they still saw each other regularly in Yellowknife, to have some drinks and catch up on the latest gossip of the mine. Molakoe seemed unable to detach emotionally from the mine, despite his firing, like a victim of Stockholm syndrome.

Amorak would never have confessed to Lou that he sometimes feared ending up like him, thrust aside from the path of men, changing his job for that of full-time alcoholic, living on the scant generosity of the White Man's Government. However, till now, in spite of several incidents involving violence and some sexual harassment that might have landed him some time in the Big House if the White Bosses had found out, he had managed to keep himself in the "slow cooker," as he liked to call the secret drinking at the mine, and to continue to work the inhumane twelve-hour shifts in the pit. It was only when he had a leisure week every fourteen days that he became a full-on drinker. The place of his family in this scheme of things was something he could not afford to look at too hard. Life, his own life, seemed to run as fast as a high speed train. He just held on tight to the back fender with the little sanity he had left because should he let this sliver of sanity go, the system would kick him off with such brutality that it would smash him to pieces.

When he first started at the mine, he had believed the fairytale that one could progress through the ranks, that life could be better if one worked hard and behaved acceptably. He had tried. By God he had. He had applied to courses, requested promotions, laughed at the Bosses' jokes. But a couple of years ago he had finally become conscious that there was nothing for him in the world above, the world of comfort and privilege.

He had reached the "glass ceiling" a long time ago as a heavy machinery operator in the pit. The bosses no longer answered his requests for promotion or training. They did not even dignify them with a rejection note, or one of those meetings he had attended in the earliest days, where the foreman awkwardly fidgeted with his hands and avoided his eyes with an apologetic expression on his face, as he delivered from the parapet of his metal desk, sentences like, "maybe on another occasion," or "this position does not match your profile, but I encourage you to keep on trying." Not even that now. Now they just assumed he was a big boy and he should know that the few prestigious positions belonged to the whites who sat comfortably in heated offices and slept in luxury individual suites, far from the apartments the aboriginal workers had to share. No, there would be no more promotions for Amorak Whitefox. No more progress. His life was in that pit within the frozen earth, where one felt more dead than alive, where, in the ghostly light of his machine, he would endlessly extract rock; rock that belonged to his ancestors, to make the White Men rich, leaving his health in the toxic fumes and the relentless cold.

Amorak tried to remember the details of the time he had spent in the bar with Molakoe that evening. His sickly complexion, his persistent and annoying cough, his raspy laughter, his smell of tobacco and dirty clothes that clashed with the distinguished Scottish ambiance of the McKenzie Lounge. He had a few drinks with him. Whiskey for him and Captain Morgan for Lou. That he knew. They had also eaten some chicken wings but he couldn't remember what time that was. Probably it was already dark when he entered the bar. Or perhaps not. It was surely dark when he came out.

The snow curtain was growing thicker. In order not to lose the track, he had to guide himself by the dark mass of the tree wall on his left. The snowmobile was now lurching side to side, violently shoved by the wind. Driving on was unreasonable, but his mind was holding on to the idea of the refuge, as a child holds on to his favorite toy, so he kept on searching for the red light, "paff, paff, paff." Any moment, he was going to hear it or see it, he reassured himself. Any moment now… But the only answer he got was the maddening howl of the wind in his ears.

II

Women regard me now as an old man, Jimmy considered as he fell under the implacable dark stare of his daughter-in-law. The idea dug into his stomach like an ice splinter. It was quite likely that his son, his only son, was dead somewhere in the track between Rae-Edzo and Nogha Ti. How could he be thinking about such futile matters? And yet, the woman's contemptuous stare had filled him with a sudden abasement that was new to him and that, for one brief instant, had displaced any other thought in the way only the human soul's abysses are capable of doing.

Not that he had ever been a ladies' man. The skinny, weak legs and the crutches inherited from his childhood poliomyelitis would not have helped him become a Don Juan, should he have wanted to be. But never until this moment had he felt looked at by a woman as other than a man. Not a relentless hunter like his father, no, but at least a man. *An old man*, he thought, passing a rough hand over his thick white hair. And once you are an *old man*, you stop being a good businessman, or a guy who can fly an airplane, or a good trapper: You become just another old timer, just like hundreds of millions of old timers. Old age was a thing that did not recognize differences. Or did it? For sure it was supposed to. In his Dogrib culture, elders were regarded as beings with enough wisdom to have attained old age in the Arctic. That achievement in itself made them worth of being carefully watched by young men and women in order to learn the art of survival. An elder was someone in whose presence children were not allowed to run or scream. Someone who received the best parts of the game the clan hunted. An elder was that impressive character who told mysterious stories by the fire and all the kids listened without blinking. Hunter kids, kids without TV, without safety seats. Kids with scars.

The older generations still felt this awe and respect deeply engraved in their heritage, but the youth? Most had been schooled by the White Men, who absurdly enough, did not feel attached to the land, but to money and the bunches of clatter they could buy with it. Therefore the elders' wisdom was of no use to them. Other than some pitiful attempts at singing a couple of traditional songs, the schools did not teach Dogrib, so the young could no longer communicate with their own grandparents, who did not speak English, unless the old folks had "made time" at the residential schools in their own childhoods.

Anyway, there was little to communicate now, since the young were no longer interested in hunting or fishing, or in learning the arts of survival that kept their ancestors for millenniums. They lived in heated houses, ate food that they took out of cans and bags and wasted their youth in front of TVs, or even worse, with their noses stuck in a bag full of glue.

Young people were now interested in learning the art of making money, since they wanted to move in the sparkling world the White Man showed on TV. The world of the beautiful people, beautiful dresses, beautiful cars, and recorded laughter, where there was no failure, no misery, no disease. Where there was no garbage or black oil swamps tainting the forests and the seas. The millions of starving children were merely a bothersome fact that could be easily zapped out with the remote. In order to obtain a little morsel of this lie, these young generations gave in to the kingdom of money: the mortgages, the credit cards, the debt. The modern slavery. In this realm, the Dogrib were the losers. The scarce education they received was rarely enough to give them access to well paid jobs, and many ended up lost in disenchantment and alcohol.

One could see these defeated warriors on the streets of the big cities. Tattered and grey, as though they were taking up the color of the concrete in the same way they once proudly wore the colors of their lands and their beasts. Some of them wandered aimlessly, with the empty expression of men whose spirits were no longer with them. Others were still filled with the rage of having been scammed and not being able to get out from under it, because the scam was now their world, their environment, their way of life. Because they breathed and ate the scam, and it laughed at them from every show window, where they could see the reflection of their own forlorn Blackfoot, Cree, Chipewyan, Dogrib, or Deh Cho face mixed with the elegant clothes they would never wear or the computers they would never own. Still, this anger, with its danger and its darkness, was better than the nothingness of the others.

The elders witnessed this collapse helplessly and their spirits mourned, for they had known freedom. But nobody paid attention to them anymore. Not even the white elders garnered respect. For the White Man, elders were a useless bunch that only generated expense and inconvenience and should be piled, together with other elders, in old folk's homes. Those old folk's homes were all the same, as if all elders were alike and they liked exactly the same furniture, the same meals, the same games, the same TV shows. They were allowed no preferences, opinions, wishes, or dreams, as if their only duty on this planet was to occupy a room in the costly and crowded Death's waiting room. As if old age were not a stage of human experience worth living, worth being loved, revered, and appreciated, as is any form of life.

Every now and then, there was of course some recognition, like on Veteran's Day, when some elders were bestowed the yearly glory day they were due for taking part in some bloody massacre that probably colored their nightmares for life. Apart from this and a couple of other dates, nobody was interested in enjoying the healing and serene company of an elder, nor in accepting their wisdom on how to read the trace of a marten under the snow, or how to cut a tree to make it grow properly, or how to survive the spiritual unbinding of witnessing the Nazi Holocaust.

This thoughtless attitude was in contradiction with the white doctors' obsession of making elders live forever, as if death were unnatural, an aberration that should never take place. Then once it took place—and it sure did—it was hidden carefully in special buildings, and dispatched hastily and discreetly, as a package of marijuana in the presence of police.

Jimmy used to joke with his doctor, when he obstinately pressed him to stop smoking. "I'm gonna die anyway, doc," he said, laughing his raspy laugh.

"But my job consists on preventing this from happening too early and on improving your quality of life," the doctor preached, without the slightest hint of humor sense. "Tobacco is a part of my quality of life," Jimmy said with a smile, and the doctor sighed.

So, no, as things were, Jimmy did not want to be an elder, or to be regarded as one, although at his seventy-eight years, he could barely escape the dreaded label. He took a big swig of coffee, trying to shoo these images away with the intense thick flavor. Dark thoughts had a knack of growing uncontrollably like poison ivy, if one did not cut them off on time. They crept up through the bones and invaded everything, as opposed to the shiny happy thoughts, the thoughts one had to cherish, water, and weed to help them grow and stay alive.

"I'm not going to cry, if that's what you're expecting," his daughter in law, Cynthia, blurted out suddenly, and her voice sounded cold and metallic, like a fork falling on a tile floor. Still with the mug to his lips, he followed her nervous moves with his eyes. Some electric force seemed to compel her to pass a cloth again and again over the clean kitchen counter, and her whole body convulsed in this sterile exercise. Jimmy felt a profound sympathy for this woman, whose Indian face had been forged to express the utter unhappiness she had been suffering for years. The unyielding cold light of the fluorescent tube hardened her already bitter complexion to ugliness.

Beyond the window, the moon caressed with a subtle blue tinge the snow on Nogha Ti roofs, over which the smoke of the chimneys rose gently, like the breath of a sleeping beast. Everything rested with a serenity that seemed to deny the howling blizzard that had engulfed the village some hours ago, seizing, perhaps, his son as a prey. It was a mystery whether he had survived or not, since the track had not been cleared yet to allow a search party. *The sky seemed calm enough now for a helicopter*, he thought, squinting at the stars.

Whatever the outcome was, one thing was for sure: in a few hours, even before dawn, the whole village would pass by the house to support the likely widow who, as announced, was not going to cry. All five hundred inhabitants, or at least the Dogrib, since the less than twenty whites who worked in the administration, the school and the health center lived in their own ghetto and rarely got involved in local tragedies, would drop by the house. They would have to welcome them and give them bannock, tea, caribou, and dry fish. The women would bring the big pots with food, just as they had at so many other mournings, and would busy themselves at the kitchen while the men would sit silently sipping tea in the living room. It was not necessary to say anything, just to be there.

Later they would go to the small blue log church and would pray some resigned prayers. It was not going to be an easy day at any cost. He was pretty sure that his granddaughter Jiewa was not going to be kind to the visitors either, since the natural Dogrib sense of comradeship and solidarity had been contaminated for her with the White Man's false concept of "charity." A charity that is humiliating for those who receive it. But there was more to Cynthia and Jiewa's sourness. There was a hell of a lot more; he had to admit for the sake of fairness. There was a world of dark underground mazes behind the ragged bitterness of the house. A world he had cowardly—cautiously, was how he chose to name his behavior—chosen not to explore and now it would burst open in all its power, like a doomed tomb or an unhealed wound.

Jimmy rubbed his worn-out eyes; they were throbbing and hot under his heavy eyelids. He knew the kind of conversation his daughter-in-law was searching for and it was too painful for him, especially in that moment, so he did not answer. He could not fathom the depth of the misery his son had sunk in to deserve losing the right to be mourned by his family. The darkness invited him like a teasing specter. "You know," it whispered. "You know very well, don't you? You have always known." And yes, perhaps he *had* always known, but now he did not feel capable of descending into the mazes. Not yet. Not tonight.

There had always been plenty of silence between him and his daughter-in-law, but that one was dense like seal blood. Jimmy sipped his coffee, turned his head to the window and let his tired eyes linger in the snow, trying to read the possibility that his son was still alive. But the dark crystal returned the faint reflection of his face, depleted and made old by anguish, and the blurry movement of the woman fluttering around aimlessly like a moth around a light bulb.

Jimmy wondered, not without a dose of resentment, how a young woman could be so bitter. If Amorak had made her so unhappy, why did she not leave him? Divorce was not unheard of among their people. In fact, ever since women had been properly informed of their civil rights, it had become a rather popular practice. And yet she had chosen to stay in that—how did they call it these days? Was it dysfunctional?—marriage, in that house without laughter. If his son was to blame for that sour expression, why had she never considered leaving him? What the hell, she was young; she might have taken the kids, started anew. Jimmy himself would have helped them; she had to know he would have. What kind of excuses did she come up with to keep her in that unhappy place? Perhaps she had fallen apart with Amorak and her spirit had not come back. Or perhaps the wounds had scarred so roughly that she could no longer feel life. But talking about what one might have done or what one wishes had not done are useless. So no, he was not going to answer. Not now, probably not ever.

How urgent it feels to solve all problems when death shows its pointy ears, Jimmy thought. The deceptive clockwork of our minds does not stop mulling on stuff that could have been done better, as though the past were a mere rehearsal, a draft or a sketch which we could redo with the due corrections. But as it is, life has the ugly habit of writing with permanent ink. In spite of his disability, Jimmy justified to himself, he had taught Amorak, as best as he could, to hunt and fish. He had instructed him in the basics of survival, but in the end he had lost him to the mainstream of his generation and agreed to let him grow without respect or communion with the Earth. How could someone, in such a tough environment, not respect and fear Nature? He did not understand that. For what reason did they think they were going to be saved? What rare enchantment did they believe they possessed that would keep them harmless despite foolish inattention to the dangers? He had always considered that mankind's ambition to be enriched, or even to survive, by disrespecting and hurting the Planet, was an incomprehensible paradox, but especially in this place, in the Arctic.

Jimmy shook his head in disbelief and frustration. For years he had seen his son reject his own roots and play the White Man's game in order to earn a well remunerated job at the diamond mines, from which he came home once every two weeks exhausted, jaded, loaded with bootlegged booze and ready to get hammered for the few leisure days his job allowed him. Somehow he had believed Amorak would change. At some point he had to mature and take responsibility, after all he was a father and a husband. Sadly, this change had never taken place.

At first, when the white men were just getting established in the region, Jimmy had rejoiced that his offspring would never have to walk the taiga with their dog sleds searching for game and fishing, seeing their children die from diseases or hypothermia, as his own ancestors had. Then he had discovered the lie and found out that the anxiety of the caribou hunt or the lake trout fishing had been replaced by the anguish of the mortgage and the car loan and the credit cards. Maybe the ghost of death by frost was now far back among his people's fears, but there was slavishness and emptiness in the sterile pursuits of these new men, who had forgotten how to play the drums as one, or how to fill their lungs with the vivifying smell of the first early spring dawns.

On the other hand, his generation, the "old timers," had been brought up as nomad hunters, living in tents, in communion with freeze and famine. They had known the white men—few in those times—they had contracted their diseases with catastrophic results, but there had not been much money, that was for sure. The Hudson Bay posts were based on barter, giving them ammunition, flour, tea, tobacco, nails, and canvas in exchange for the furs they brought back from hunting. Only rarely was money handled and even then, it returned to the Whites' hands at an amazing speed. Like these days. Yeah, not much had changed. Way back then, he had seen the bosses throw a complimentary bottle of whiskey in with the groceries, as a good will gesture. That was how alcohol gradually seeped into their people's lives like poison.

Jimmy evoked the memory of his father, when he was the young hunter, proudly refusing the bottle that the boss, displaying his blackened teeth in a smile, was offering him. He just shook his head once, in a simple incontestable gesture, he collected the groceries with his powerful arms and left on the counter the bundle of glossy furs his mother had so craftily tanned, and the boss's blackened smile dissolved into a resentful expression when he saw him leave the cabin, young, strong, unwavering.

Nowadays, things had changed dramatically. The White Men still sold the alcohol and harvested huge amounts of money in taxes from it, but on the other hand, they spent millions in producing pamphlets and sending Health Employees to convince people not to buy it. Everyone had to be indoctrinated into the new system and the White Men carefully oversaw that they were, through armies of Social Services, Health, and Police. But the watch was not being very thorough, or perhaps the system was too faulty, since so many slipped through it like water through a basket, into the hands of alcohol, drugs and disenchantment.

Jimmy's eyes automatically focused on a window that had been lit up in a nearby cabin. *Not yet, please*, he pleaded from his heart. The village was waking up and soon people would start to show up for support. He feared exposing his burning pain to all as much as he had feared as a child exposing his sickly legs and his crutches. He looked at the time on the round white kitchen clock. It was only four thirty. Probably it was only someone going to the bathroom, he thought with relief. There was still time. Not much, but he did not want to spend it in that kitchen flooded with hate. He could do nothing to alleviate that hate and he did not want it turned on him either.

His granddaughter's smile warmed up his heart momentarily from her old picture stuck to the fridge door with a fruit shaped magnet. In the photo she must have been about ten. She was wearing a tattered parka and she had a protective arm around her little brother Edzo. They were both squinting at the early spring sun reflected in the snow, which made them look angry.

Or were they actually angry? Jiewa, his granddaughter. Had he lost her, too? Chances were yes; he had, when he had not been there in the moment when she needed him most. When she had asked him the unthinkable and he had to say "no," and face the child's deceived expression as she saw her old timer hero fall into the bottomless abyss of disappointment. And even through the painful memory of her devastated expression, he still resisted the idea of losing her. It just couldn't happen. Perhaps there was still a chance for him to form a bridge of unconditional love that she could not refuse. Perhaps if he could bare his soul for her... He had to try, before it was too late. If it wasn't already. He finished the rest of his cold coffee and stood up, feeling on his bones the full weight of his seventy-eight years.

Jiewa's bedroom was a perfect teenage mess. The walls were covered with posters depicting frantic excessive characters covered in tattoos and sweat that looked right out of a Halloween dance. There was a mountain of clothes of several days on the chair by the desk, evidence that nobody ever sat there to study. The carpeted floor was covered with shoes, stuffed animals, and empty chips bags.

On her twin bed, the girl slept peacefully. The warm cereal smell of sleeping children still emanated from his teenage granddaughter and the violet light that seeped through the curtains bathed the round girlish face of his little Jiewa. Jimmy caressed the glossy black hair that spread over the pillow framing her face like a halo of darkness. He smiled at the baby he could still see in her and allowed himself to stop his anguish to relish this moment. If he could just stay like that indefinitely, just watching her, breathing in her peace, as if no evil had been done, as though nothing bad was going to happen.

"Before the news arrives, I have many things to tell you," said the old man from his heart. "Things I have never told you before, because I thought it was not necessary for you to know, because after all they are already in your blood and in your spirit. But today you may be waking up to your father's death and I fear that, like your mother, you will not cry. The rage of not crying for the death of a father seems to me more painful than crying. Resentment wounds stink much more than loss wounds. This I know because I am an old man covered in scars and when they tell me that my son is dead, I am going to be even older and broken, and you will be awake, with your wild eyes full of fire and you will not want to hear these old tales, nor will I probably be in the mood to tell them. And although you are now asleep and I am talking without words, I believe our souls are talking. Word conversations are normally good for nothing. They just ruffle the silence of the bush and scare the game. And after all, nobody listens. Or almost nobody.

"I know you have lost your faith in me. I am not going to try to justify myself, or to sell you my truth. I just want you to know where that pain come from. Our clan's pain. My pain. I don't expect you to understand, because you are in the age of feeling, not of understanding, but I know my words will come back to you when you are ready.

"Now, in spite of love and family bonds, there is an abyss between us, since your generation and mine are alien to each other. Your feelings, your dreams, your thoughts, are flooded with deafening music and strange talk from a universe of electronics that isolates you from old geezers like me. I understand this is what the White Man sells to you children these days, but I don't seem to comprehend it. Even though I read their books in my time and understood the language of the white men's hearts, I have my roots and my feelings here, where my body lives, in the forest, in the familiar song of the wind, in the branches loaded with snow, in the vibration of the drums and the scent of the tanned hide.

"But I do know the white men. Their permanent inner fight. I even knew the love of a white woman. Yeah, believe it or not. With my pitiful skinny legs and my crutches, I had once a white girlfriend. And what a woman. I will never forget her, because it was with her that I experienced the emotions I had read in all those books. The stormy love of the white woman, her peculiar vision of life, her delicacy and sophistication, the complexity of all she expects from life. No less, yeah. White men expect things from life, as if life were a provider, more or less trustworthy, at their service. And if they don't receive what they expected, they get frustrated and sad and they mourn the injustice of their predicament. How can life be fear or unfair, Jiewa? This attitude, which would seem in principle so childish and stupid, leads them to a way of sadness they transform into art, writing, painting, loving. Especially loving. They create imaginary universes for passion, anger, nostalgia, jealousy. No, Jiewa, I won't forget my white woman. I keep her asleep and tucked in in a cozy corner of my memory, but she sometimes wakes up when I read a romance novel, or when I hear some music we used to dance to together.

"This was when I was about thirty something. Before I met your grandma, of course, make no mistake. I had already started making some money with the grocery store and I often travelled on business to Yellowknife, where I sometimes went into the white men's bars, accompanied by white men of course. Don't think that was the norm in that time. Back then, when a Dogrib went to Yellowknife, we called it *Somba K'e*—place where the money is—to sell furs and get ammunition, groceries, and tobacco, he tread carefully, got what he needed and left hastily, for everybody understood he had no business overstaying. But my tradesman status and my knowledge of English gave me the chance to socialize with white men, mostly because of the curiosity they felt about me, but to tell you the truth, I enjoyed it. Isn't it something that being born in the middle of the Taiga I turned out to be a party man? Not a heavy drinker, but definitely a party man," Jimmy mused with a dreamy smile on his face.

"In those bar evenings I got to explore underground facets of the white men's nature. Some, when they get drunk, release their inner child, naughty and fun. They sing, laugh, hug each other, tell spicy jokes and one wonders why aren't they like that all the time. Others get sad, sink their heads upon the bar counter, as though offering their neck to be cut with an axe, and one wonders what the hell do they drink for. Others become hostile and dark; their gaze turns grimy and their undisclosed racist thoughts come to the surface like a putrid second skin, and one thinks, this guy might kill me in any moment. In any case, drinking with the white men, I have observed, is the best way of getting to know their true nature. Which comes in handy for business.

"Me, I didn't say much during those long evenings. I just sat at the table with them, drank with them, and watched them with a concealed eagerness. Anyway, being an Indian, nobody expected me to say much. Just to feel thankful for the honor of being allowed to sit at their table. Since I have never been a talkative man, I felt at ease in that role. And as it happens, it was in one of those bars, the Wild Cat Cafe, that I met her. She was older than me, but I don't know exactly how much, because I never had the nerve to ask her age. See, those were other times. We're talking forty years ago here. Things were done otherwise back then. But she was very beautiful, not like the spooks you have in your posters. She was attractive and elegant. She gave off an energy that one could see hundreds of yards away, like a forest fire.

"That night there was a group crammed up in one end of the log cabin that was—and still is—the Wild Cat, playing something that wanted to sound like jazz and the place was packed, sunk in smoke and voices that strived to rise over the music, as if any conversation deserved to be listened to above those songs. I was sitting at a table with a group of bank workers with whom I had just had a business meeting. They were boring people, but booze was starting to make them more and more interesting.

"Then she entered the bar. She caught my eye from the very moment she came through the door, shaking the snow off her coat and stomping her boots. Not that she was spectacularly beautiful, surely nothing like that bunch of skinny heavy breasted blondes you look up to, that seem to have come out of the very same mold. She had a gaze and a presence that seemed to drag all the spirits in her wake. Life breathed through her with such a compelling power I couldn't keep my eyes off her.

"She made her way through the crowd and the smoke to sit down with a friend that was waiting for her. Both ladies were in their early forties, that age in which women have either fallen in a resigned impersonal sluggishness, or have discovered the freedom of doing and saying whatever they want. She belonged to this second type, ostentatiously so.

"At some point, our stares met somewhere in the smoke and the music; mine remained permanently ensnared, like that of an idiot, I suspect, hers coming and going like a butterfly, but intent, unequivocal, bold. She did not try to disguise her interest in me, but I did not make an attempt to approach her. Those were not times of equality, Jiewa. One had to be extremely careful not to offend a white man, let alone a white lady. I would never have had the audacity to address her in any way. I would just have remained at my table, relishing her presence and her magnetism from a prudent distance, breathing her aura of freedom and strength, resisting the attraction and daydreaming. So, when I saw her say goodbye to her friend and walk towards me with firm gait, drawing her court of spirits and sparks like a queen's cloak, I started to shake and a part of me wanted to run away and scream at the cold starry night, but her ease and firmness kept me in place. She knew all the men that were with me, so she had no difficulty to join our table, plunging fearlessly into the boring conversation they were having and handling naturally the finance terms and concepts that sounded Chinese to me. One by one, the rest of the men left for rowdier tables, or went back home to their wives. The last one offered her a drive home, but she declined with a smile, so there was only her and I.

"Then she stood up and sat down beside me. Not in front of me, but beside me, see? Oh, she smelled of expensive perfume, lotion and tobacco.

"'My name is Veronique Leduc,' she said offering a firm and warm hand. Only then did I notice that my table fellows had not deemed it appropriate to introduce us. We talked and drank for more than two hours, but time just flew for us. She told me about her personal history: her sadly civilized divorce, the lost years as a cheated inmate housewife, her plans to travel and enjoy her life with the very considerable amount of money her husband had to give her in spite of himself. She asked me about myself and she listened with genuine attention to the few pieces of information I blurted out nervously. I noticed she listened like a Dogrib, without interrupting, without getting uneasy, without desperately trying to fit in her comments, as the white men normally do.

"Suddenly we realized that around us there were only three or four stubborn silent patrons, immersed in dark conversations with their glasses. The waiters had begun to sweep, putting the chairs upside down on the tables. She looked at me with a totally new frighteningly beautiful stare.

"'You come to my house?' She did not say *to have a cup of coffee,* or *to see my silver spoon collection.* No. She just said, 'You come to my house?' The world then started to spin very fast around me to the rhythm of my uncontrolled heart. Suddenly, the same shadow that had been pursuing me throughout my life fell over me. The fear of showing my pathetic handicapped body, the fear of rejection, the memory of children's cruel laughter. But she read me like an open book and passed me my crutches with a smile and we started off.

"We made love with teenagers' passion, without words, without explanations. The following morning, I decided not to head back home, as I had planned. I had to stay a couple more days, because I did not feel capable of parting from that power of Nature. The couple more days became a week, at the end of which, there was a bond between us, so special and powerful that it has never been broken, even though now we do not see or talk to each other any more.

"I felt like a seventeen year old boy in love, greedily, voraciously, with wings on my heels and on my heart. When the moment to leave could not be postponed any longer, I explained to her, standing in front of the airplane, shaking like a child, holding her gloved hands with my sweaty hands, that I was afraid of losing her, terrified that she might forget me, that everything would be over if I left to tend to my business. I did not know how to express my love to her, my need of her, and I feared that, if I could not tie her with words, like the novel heroes did, she would vanish like a mirage. But Veronique laughed straightforwardly, throwing her head back, as she always did. She held my hand firmly and said, 'Just go tend your business without a worry, cause this lady's heart, you're wearing it!' and to my amazement, she led my hand to her left breast, over her fur coat. 'But come back soon, eh? Don't keep me waiting,' she warned raising her small hand. And she kissed me right there, in public.

"And did I ever come back. We saw each other at least twice a month for more than one year, always with that teenage craze for each other, the breathless words, and the yearning moans. Don't you tell your grandma, but many a time I have missed the passion of the white woman, the tide of pleasure, jealousy, craziness, tenderness, sadness, anger. That emotional rollercoaster they need as a fuel for happiness. That almost material strength that raises you to heaven and then drags you through the ice. Perhaps it is because of the novels they read and the movies they watch, or perhaps the novels and the movies are like that because of them. Who knows? I didn't ask too much, because I was back to the age of feeling, not understanding. And hell if I needed to understand a thing.

"One day she came with the news that she wanted to go to Las Vegas with me. Travelling in those days was not as cheap and easy as now and although I made a good living out of my business, I could not afford too much luxury, especially when I was flying regularly to Yellowknife to see her. So she offered to pay for my expenses. I did not think this was appropriate and I strongly refused, but she was adamant about this idea of the travel, and she was very upset. She started to scream at me. That I was not able to make an effort to satisfy her, that she was excited about traveling with me and why did I had to be such a party pooper?

"I gave it a second thought then. I knew money was not an issue for her and all I wanted was to make her happy, so I reluctantly agreed to the crazy plan. She bought the tickets, booked the hotel and helped me with the tedious paperwork to obtain a passport. I went through the process like a sleepwalker, feeling I was being taken, rather than walking on my own. I just wondered, annoyed, why did she have to get the Las Vegas bug, when we were so comfy in her house in Yellowknife, where I already knew where the glasses and the pans were, where I did not feel like a stranger. All I knew of Las Vegas I had seen it on the movies, or read in in the pulp novels. A surreal neon lighted place in the middle of a scorching desert where there was nothing but casinos and hotels, prostitutes and gamblers, gangsters and killers. Frankly, it did not sound tempting at all to me. It did not call me as it seemed to call Veronique.

"We had to take four flights to get there. Veronique guided me with ease and patience through the big airports, the customs routines, the waiting areas. I, who still wondered at the idea of flying, stayed in a permanent daze, with the uncomfortable feeling that I was living someone else's dream, enjoying colors, smells and tastes that did not belong to me.

"I admit that our arrival in Las Vegas caught me by surprise. I had a total meltdown at the vision of that colorful nest of lights in the middle of the desert darkness, the massiveness of the hotels, the excess of the casinos, the living stream of people in the streets, the luxury, the fake sensation of security. The white men's paradise, I thought. It didn't matter if they won or lost, they just walked in a permanent state of greedy hallucinated grace that was very contagious.

"With awe I regarded this prodigy of a city from the taxi that was driving us from the airport to the hotel, marveling at that sour sweet alien beauty. Veronique looked at me sideways with her rascally smile.

"'I knew it would leave you speechless. That's what happens with Las Vegas. One is never ready to see it for the first time.' I laughed and I answered I didn't think I would be ready for the second time either.

"We stayed on the fifteenth floor of an impressive hotel. From its glass walls you could see the whole city with its neon-covered constructions, its avenues where car lights flew like the luminous blood of the city. I could have stayed there, by that magic glass wall, for hours, days. But we went out to have supper at a restaurant that must have been very expensive, although I don't know for sure, because she didn't let me see the bill. Then of course, we went on a casinos tour and I started to feel vertigo. Can you imagine your grandpa, right out of the bush, smelling of rawhide, with the looks and the clothes of a Dogrib hunter, strolling through the casinos in Las Vegas? Ah, you would have had quite the laugh to see me there so disoriented and outlandish. She, with her patience and with a happiness that was almost euphoria, explained to me the rules of the games while she pleasantly lost money on each of them.

"I hardly spoke. I just let her carry me through that dreamland regarding her as a goddess smug in her fairy kingdom, naturally handling magical words, shiny objects, making dreams and nightmares come true. When we were finally back in our glass bedroom it was almost dawn, but the maddened fever, the rivers of lights, the huge neon signs did not stop vibrating. I guess daydreamers have no schedules. Especially in Las Vegas.

"I stood by the glass, where I could see the city lights and the reflection of Veronique sitting at the dresser, removing her makeup.

"'You have been very quiet,' she said, looking at me from the mirror. 'Tell me what do you think of all this?'

"I shrugged. Her moves, I noticed, were harmonious and serene even in the most lackluster routines, and I was already admiring her image, mingled with the maddened dance of lights in the dark crystal, with some kind of nostalgia or loss. For this was her world and the other one, that of caribou hunting, the wolves and the bears, the blizzards and the drums, was mine. Where could the souls of two opposed universes meet? I would never belong in hers and she would never belong in mine. We had always known, but that night, in front of that prodigious and terrible dark glass, I was forced to accept it. I didn't say anything because I knew that this trip, my sort of baptism in her world, meant a lot to her, and I could not stand the idea of making her cry.

"The fact is, after our return, things cooled down fast between us; we started to move from each other slowly but painfully.

There were, for the first time, uncomfortable silences, excuses and unwillingness. I started to space my visits out further and further and, since she did not complain, I imagined she had reached the same conclusion as me. Perhaps she was seeing someone else, for she could not live without love. This thought gave me a pang of jealousy, but no resentment. I understood. I remember the last time I saw her, three months after the trip. We met at the Wild Cat, the same place where I saw her for the first time, and she informed me with few words and hardly looking at me that she was moving to Vancouver. I understood this, too. How long can a fish stay alive out of the water? That day we did not go to her house after supper. She said she was very tired and she had to do a lot of packing. I nodded without insisting, actually longing to return to my hotel room and drink a whole bottle of whisky on my own. It is so sad to attend the funeral of a passion.

"And that's it. We never saw each other again. I keep her phone number, but I never call her and she doesn't call either. Perhaps she is dead. At our age the possibility is always there, but I don't think so. She had so much life in her that it should last her for many years. Her light was not like a sparkler, that shines brightly and dies soon, but powerful and serene, like a star. I remember her attractive face, her ballerina harmony and her aura of passion. And I'm sure she would love to know that I remember her like that, the playful little thing." Jimmy laughed at the memories.

"It is a shame that it could not be, but no feeling is ever wasted. People who tell you that are resentful or outright stupid. Veronique made me see the world through her eyes, taught me how a white woman feels, proved that the adventures I had read in all those novels were not lies, that the warmth and the madness existed, as reported by Dumas, Tolstoy, Shakespeare, Hemingway. Her passion for life made me explore regions of my soul that would be in the dark without her. For all this I will be eternally grateful to her, even though many of the things she showed me were at the other side of the abyss.

"And you, my Jiewa, my little one, in which of both worlds do you live?" Jimmy smiled, barely touching the soft face of his sleeping granddaughter. "Do you want to be a rock star, like the spooks on your wall? But no, you are still a Dogrib," he whispered, frowning with pride. "Not only because you have black slanted eyes, brown skin, and glossy black hair but because you are my granddaughter. Your blood is the blood of my people. You have the wisdom that makes paths in the snow, the unwavering courage that the bear identifies and respects. You are definitely a Dogrib and your almond face, no matter how angry, understands my wrinkled face without speaking, as it understands the air around it and the sounds of the bush. It is going to be hard for you to find your soul, Jicwa. Even though it is right here, where you are right now. You will have to dig hard in the lies they have dumped on you for years and when you find it, believe it or not, it will spring up shiny and new, like a bride's gown."

"What do you dream now, my girl, while your father, my son, travels? Look for your soul, my love, look for your roots. You are going to need them to understand and defeat the pain of your people. Your pain."

IV

"As a child, I had polio," Jimmy continued. "This is no mystery to you because you have heard me tell the story a hundred times, and you roll your eyes, impatient. Always so impatient. You know I would have died, as all crippled beings die here, if I hadn't been spotted by one of those missionaries. Way back then there was not a health center, or a church, or a school. There was not even a village here. Nogha Ti was just the place where the Hudson Bay's post was. A log cabin where the Dogrib came to exchange their furs for ammunition, traps, nails, sugar, tea, flour, tobacco, and whatnot. That's why a lot of people camped here and it slowly became a meeting place. Dances by the fire were organized for the youth to meet each other and marry out of their families, to bear healthier and stronger children. Inflated stories about huntings were told and those who had died were honored.

"People then started to stay permanently, especially during the fishing season, when there was not much to do but tend to the nets in the lake, smoke the trout and prepare a good provision of food and clothes for the winter. By the time winter began, we packed up and left, our sleds loaded with provisions, our dogs lustrous after a summer of feasting on fish. We traveled after the caribou herds. Wherever they went, that was where we went, for they were our livelihood. We also trapped for furs to exchange at the Company.

"The clans worked as teams in which every single person had a mission: the elders and the women took care of small children and instructed them. They picked up berries, tanned furs and made coats with them, smoked meat. Others trapped, some cut the meat and took it to the camp, still others prepared the tents and covered their floors with soft branches, others collected firewood. The clan had to stay together because each person was key for the other members' survival. There were times of hunger, when we could not find game or fishing. Sometimes people weakened and died, they extinguished slowly as the cold took possession of their bodies. Hunger is a terrible thing. You can't imagine how it can change people." Jimmy shook this thought from his mind. "But never mind. I don't believe you will ever experience it. The true hunger. The one that kills. Anyway. When we came back in the summer to the Company's post, we noticed there were more and more people gathered there. Our people needed the white man's things and commerce had become a fundamental part in the Dogrib's lives.

"It was then that the priests arrived. The two missionaries that would save my life later on. They came four or five times a year, coinciding with Christmas, Easter, Thanksgiving and other important events, like baptisms or first communions. A small airplane left them there with provisions for one week and picked them up as soon as the weather conditions allowed, which was often three or four weeks later than scheduled. We fed them with dry caribou and smoked fish, and also fresh meat, when there was some to spare; but they did not like that food and they had very sad faces as they dutifully chewed the tough meat. They were not happy sleeping in the tents either. They were too cold and got sick easily. To be honest, although their arrival was earnestly expected, it was also feared in a way, because we knew if one of them died, the police would rain on us and someone would likely have to pay for the tragedy. So were things way back then. Luckily the missionaries proved to be more resilient than we reckoned, for none of them died. At least not in Nogha Ti.

"The thing is, with time, according to an implicit order of the Canadian Government, we all became Catholic and the visits of those priests became the most important social event for our people, even above our drum dance, which the missionaries rejected angrily as Devil's worship. Upon their arrival, those who were in town, hastily took dogs and sleds and went out to look for people who were in the bush hunting. There were those who, at the sight of the airplane, travelled several days in order to attend the masses. Until the church was finished, mass was celebrated in a tent, where those men in black long robes gathered us and, through very long and terrifying sermons, tried to keep us away from inbreeding, polygamy, child abuse, and other many horrors that, according to those men, would lead us directly to the flames of Hell. We listened to them in a mute stupor, amazed at their clothing, their pale faces, the strange luggage they brought along, the precious bejeweled dishes and glasses they handled during their ceremonies with reverence, as if they were magical objects, the fascinating arcane rites they performed with severe expressions on their faces. And it was perhaps the feverish passion they put into these rituals that made us regard them as aliens and respect them, since their sermons, dictated in a practically incomprehensible Dogrib, were barely grasped by some of us, at best.

"Those rudimentary masses were our first contact with Catholicism, in which we were all baptised without understanding what was actually happening to us. And it was in one of those masses that one of the priests spotted me. I realized at once and panicked. I thought that the man had probably realised I was a useless child and would want to sacrifice me like Jesus, or something like that. By then, my disease was sufficiently critical to be noticed. My drooling, spasms and my increasing inability to walk made me a pathetic creature my parents had given up any hope of.

"The missionary, a scrawny severe man with feverish eyes and long bony hands, approached my mom after the mass. I was frozen in horror. He asked for my name in a pitiful yet understandable Dogrib, but I was not able to utter a word. Then he took my hand and repeated his name several times, very slowly, 'Faa-ther Tyyyy-roone… Faa-ther Tyyyy-roone.' In spite of the skeletal and powerful long fingers, his hand was warm and his toothy smile was broad and sincere, not the ugly showcase of rotten teeth that is most white men's smile, or used to be back then. Why, it seemed that, after all, maybe the man did not mean to sacrifice me. Then he addressed my mom, who was standing beside me, in a mixture of Dogrib and English that she listened to warily, frowning.

"'Madam, your son is very ill. I believe it is polio. We have seen other cases in the area recently.' My mom shrugged, without understanding a word. He continued, speaking slower and louder, as if the volume of his voice were going to make it easier for her to understand. It would have been hilarious, had I not been deathly afraid.

"'If we don't take him to a hospital as soon as possible, he will die,' he said, without realizing, or caring about the fact that I was listening. Or perhaps the effort of expressing himself was too overwhelming for him to take my feelings into consideration. I looked at my mom, alarmed at this news. She shrugged again.

She had never seen a hospital. Didn't know what the man was talking about. Me neither, of course. The first white men we had seen were the factors of the Company and the priests. There was a long silence.

"'Madam,' the priest proceeded, 'if I take your son with me now, he has a chance to survive, do you understand?'"

"After listening to the same sentence several times, my mother finally understood, or perhaps she understood the first time but she was giving herself time to digest the news. What she could not figure out was how the man could possibly save the weak faulty creature that she had given birth to, who clung to her desperately for sheer life. She had seen several children die. Sometimes it turned out like that. If they were not all right, death took them away without excuses. She had never thought there were alternatives to such a simple fact, so she stood there, staring at the priest, studying his face in search of a lie or mockery, but she only saw true concern and interest. Then she looked at me, her six-year old son, who seemed to shrink and stiffen day by day, suffering painful spasms that were the presage to an imminent death.

"'Perhaps we can save your son,' the priest insisted, raising his voice a notch, as if that was going to make my mother react in a more predictable way, more in accordance with the sentiment of white women. 'But he needs to come with us in the plane, to Somba K'e," he said pointing at the sky with his big flat palm pointing down. 'To the Yellowknife hospital, do you understand? It is his only chance.'

"My mother, who by then had understood perfectly, quickly shuffled her options. She did not want to see me die. She had already seen one of her sons die, a newborn the wolves took away while she was cutting wood in the bush. The image chased her day and night, made her heart jump. She felt the sharp teeth of the wolf in her own body every morning when she woke up to the real world. Ever since she had realized I was ill, she started to fear she would have to endure the loss of another child and she did not believe she would survive it. So that day she ran to my father, who was outside, hooking the dogs to go back to our camp at two days travel, where my grandma awaited. My mom repeated to him the priest's offer. He looked at both of us with resentment, as if blaming us both for my inadequacy, or for her having kept me alive for so long, a flagrant proof of his failed fatherhood. He turned back to his packing and nodded briskly just once, without looking at us, as he started tying our blankets to the sled. In that moment he considered me dead. In fact, I believe he had made that assumption a long time before.

"My mom shoved me back into the priest's tent.

"'Will he come back?' she asked him coolly.

"'We hope so,' he answered, striving to infuse some tenderness and encouragement into my mom's soul. 'I can't guarantee it, though. And I can't say when,' he added with a sad sweet smile that transformed his face completely. 'The child seems to be very sick. He will need a long treatment and then some rehabilitation to be able to walk again. He will be in good hands, though. I myself will be taking care of him, I give you my word. Besides, I will still be coming to Nogha Ti and will give you news about his progress.'

"My mother just barely understood this bunch of promises. She did not understand the meaning of giving your word, since she had never needed that to be trusted.

"Also, she would not have been able to tell the priest about the spiritual cancer that devoured her day after day since the wolves took away little Edzo, but she knew that she would not survive it again. If she saw me die, amidst spasms, screams and drooling, her spirit would disappear forever and she would never again laugh or feel the sun on her skin. After a moment's hesitation, she shoved me towards the man and she went outside to pack my clothes.

"I remember the terror of seeing them leave in the sled without me. In spite of my screams and my crying, as the scrawny dark Father Tyrone held me with his bony long fingers, whispering some reassuring words I could not understand. They held me practically prisoner in the tent, guarding me so that I did not escape, creeping painfully on my deformed body.

"A couple of days later, an airplane landed in Nogha Ti to pick us up. The priests packed hastily as they heard the noise of the engines in the sky, happy to finally be rid of the meals of tough dry caribou and the bitter cold. Then the factor came out of the post and shouted at everyone to empty the only street in the settlement for the airplane was bound to land any moment. It landed in a terrible roar and a cloud of snow dust, and before I had time to think about it, we were being hoisted up to the tiny door and getting ready to take off. Needless to say that would be the first time I was on an airplane. The priests forced me inside as I fought, maddened, as roughly as my paralysis allowed. It was a small ski airplane. I will never forget the weightlessness sensation in my stomach as we were airborne. My moaning, that had not stopped since my parents left me behind, was briskly interrupted by a gasp as I saw the land the way an eagle would, from the sky. The frozen lake, the tents that looked tiny, the bush with its trails thin like yarn. The rest of the world disappeared and the magic of flying took me over in such a way it never let go. Not till today.

"'Ain't it quite something, eh, boy?' said father Tyrone with that toothy smile that warmed up his face. And it was. Hell, it was.

"I thought those men were perhaps taking me to that Heaven they spoke so much about, but no. Yellowknife was where they were taking me. I was hospitalized there for a long time. I don't even know for exactly how long, because one does not feel the passing of seasons in the white men's heated buildings. I can only say that I came to regard it as my new home. It was a massive building—or at least that is how it looked to me—with long corridors where cold drafts whistled eerily at night. The rooms were spacious with high ceilings and they had a smell of disinfectant that it took me a long time to get used to.

"At first, I spent most of the time in a timeless lethargy, lying under the bed, listening to the rustle of the nuns' starched skirts and the squeak of the nurses' rubber soles coming and going on the hardwood floor. With time, I started to venture out of my hideout more often and I ended up getting used to sleeping on the bed, to the inactivity, the moaning that came from people languishing in adjacent rooms and the inflexible routines of the place.

"Since I was there for the long haul, the kids occupying the two other beds in my room kept rotating and I, as a veteran, explained proudly the peculiarities of the place to the newcomers: I informed them which nuns were more pleasant, and those that were more prone to administer beatings for no reason. I captained them on night expeditions through the dark drafty corridors to the waiting room by the entrance, where we checked out the pretty ladies in the colourful magazines and then tiptoed to the kitchen, where we stole cookies or cheese and hid under the table to eat them hastily. Oh, did they ever taste good, those forbidden treats," Jimmy laughed at the memory.

"When we were alone, we spoke our own language, Dogrib, which was strictly forbidden to us otherwise, under the penalty of washing your tongue with soap. Whenever a child stayed for a long period of time, we developed a strong comradeship. We swore friendship to each other and we felt invincible, like the heroes in the comic books.

"On one occasion, I shared my bedroom—I had ended up considering it MY bedroom—with an Inuvialuit child. Because of the language difference, we had to speak our bad English and some words that sounded alike in both languages, which we celebrated with laughter. They had hauled him from Tuktoyaktuk to enlist him in the residential school, but soon after the move, he had developed an unknown disease that was slowly consuming him.

"'He says that he wants to go back home to his mom,' I told the nurse who had come to wash him.

"'Well, that is not going to be possible,' she answered with a nasal musical voice, "'He is sick and he needs to stay here until he feels better,' she said, nodding satisfied at her own speech.

"'But he's not going to feel better,' I said. 'He's dying.' The nurse, who was leaving the room, stopped dead and turned around, looking at me in disbelief.

"'How can you say that?' She hollered, crossing herself as though in presence of the Devil himself. 'Wait until I tell Father Tyrone.' And she left the room in a rush of starched white skirts.

"And she honored her threat, for when Father Tyrone came to visit that afternoon, he took me out of the bedroom to the waiting room. He made me sit on the sofa and he brought a chair to sit in front of me.

"'Why did you say that to Joseph?' he asked without preamble.

"'What? That he's dying? Well, because it's true,' I answered, looking at my lap.

"'You cannot know that, young man,' said Father Tyrone wagging his long index finger in front of me. 'Only God knows the fates of men, he added for good measure.

"'Father, I am small, but I have seen enough people dying,' I answered. Father Tyrone happened to be one of the few adults whose opinion one could contest without the risk of a slap. 'It's like my grandpa, who died during a caribou hunting one winter. Or my cousin, who died giving birth to a baby in the middle of the frozen lake when we were heading for the Post. After the delivery, she started to get like Joseph and then she died.'

"'How do you mean *like Joseph?*' he asked, impatiently.

"'When you see a person's spirit already leaving,' I shrugged. 'Then they die.'

"'All right but do not mention it anymore,' said Father Tyrone with a shiver. 'That child could get very sad if he hears you.'

"'If he hears me? What? That he is going to die? He already knows, Father. He is an Indian, too.'

"Joseph died three days later, without anybody from his family coming to hug him for the last time. I sat beside him when I felt death was coming for him and I took his hand. He briefly raised his head, gave me a faint smile and let it fall back again on the pillow. 'I would like to have died in Tuktoyaktuk, with my parents, my brothers and my grandpa,' he said. I nodded in agreement. 'Do you think I will go to Heaven? Father Tyrone said I would.'

"'For sure,' I said, faking cheerfulness. 'Father Tyrone would not lie to you, you know.'

"'I guess so,' he agreed. 'It's just I always thought Heaven was only for the white men.'

"Shortly after, he was dead and his spirit was no longer with him. I pressed the bell for the nurse and went under my bed to cry. I wondered if I would also die in that building where seasons did not happen, far away from my family and my people, speaking a language that was not my own.

"I spent three days under the bed, until Father Tyrone took me out with his strong bony hands. Just as he had promised my mother, Father Tyrone never quit taking care of me. My disease kept me from attending school, but he took it on himself to teach me. Almost every afternoon, except for the times when he was out on the land, he came to visit me and he taught me to read, write, math, science, and some of the violent history of a country that, apparently, was my own. It took me many months to understand the use of learning about so many numbers and letters, formulas and dates that meant nothing to me, but I did not complain. In my time, Jiewa, children were not granted the right to complain. Complaining was intolerable and punished, so I understood pretty soon that I'd better accept the strange rhythm of life in that place, the heat of the rooms, the boring leisurely hours I had never had before, the strange bland meals, the things that, suddenly, were forbidden or sinful. I'd better accept the whole deal, because a poor handicapped Indian boy was, like anywhere else, the weakest link of the food chain.

"So I let them mold me, as they liked to call it. I read their books, that spoke about a world that was unknown to me and yet they started to trap me in their chapters loaded with adventurers, explorers, heroes always involved in some sort of quest. Their women, with complicated fancy feelings. Their ambitions and problems that had nothing to do with our day-to-day work for survival, but with an extraordinary longing for greatness, for the attainment of outlandish goals, the worth of which I could not then understand, and come to think of it, I don't think I do today, either.

"Like the sagas of suicidal expeditions that the English undertook in search for the Northern pass to bridge both sides of the American continent. Dozens of vessels sent out, only to disappear or remain stuck in the ice for years as their crews perished from hunger, cold, and desperation. You see, Jiewa, us wild people lived a nomad life in search for game and fish, accepting our environment with its threats and its gifts with gratitude, while the white men fought Nature, as if such battle were possible, imbued with a suicidal fever of fury and arrogance. I like to contemplate both positions, so radically opposed. Discrepancies like this do not give place to confusion, to grey zones. They offer a crystal clear naked truth. The North only offers these two options: acceptance or madness. You will have to make this choice, sooner or later. When you do, remember the Northern explorers, whose bodies lie uncorrupted in the eternal ice, spread all over our white geography.

"However, the choice is not easy. The mirage is very strong. The white man's grandeur illusions, which to some extent, I embraced in my youth. Their poetry, the boundless imagination that makes you travel, laugh, cry, shake. I also summed, subtracted and multiplied their numbers and, I gotta say I didn't do bad with it at all.

"With time, a true comradeship arose between Father Tyrone and I. As soon as he saw my desire to learn, a comparable desire to learn about me sprouted up in him. He asked things about our people and our traditions. I taught him Dogrib and he read me newspapers. He talked to me about politics, cinema, even the hospital's gossip which, for some reason, made him laugh until tears came to his eyes. He brought me adventure novels from the school's library and comic books that he bought with his meager pocket money. He also brought me candies and the occasional wooden toy.

"Sometimes he would sit by my bed, and then take from some pocket in his cassock a dark mysterious book. He would read from this book in a tenor voice about the frightening lives of the saints and martyrs. My favorite part was when they roasted them, beheaded them, threw them to the lions or speared them. I listened with my heart fluttering and I had atrocious nightmares at night, to the point that the nurse prohibited him to read me about any more saintly torments. He accepted this prohibition with a loud laugh, but he kept reading me the book because I asked him to. Of course he could no longer do it in his theatrical tenor voice, but in whispers and throwing stealthy glances at the door, which made it even more interesting.

"As my reading skills improved, the books the Father brought me became more and more fascinating. *Moby Dick*, *Tom Sawyer*, *The Treasure Island*, or Joseph Conrad's gripping sea stories, which I had read so many times that the pages were loose and I had to rebuild the books every time. He also taught me to play chess and backgammon and we became good friends, to the point that I sometimes forgot my stay there was temporary and that I did not—would never—belong in that world.

"In time, upon the doctor's recommendation, I was released from the hospital into a residential school, an ominous place where one's mouth felt always dry. The kids walked dismally in line through the corridors like dusty hopeless ghosts. Father Tyrone came two or three times a week to visit me. He told me to have patience, but to me patience was meant for when you were working on something, expecting something, like a caribou you have been following for several days, or trying to net a fish. But patience seemed useless to me in that place. Many of us kids didn't even know where our parents were anymore, since most of them were nomad hunters. So, where would we return when the time of patience was over? I have come across some of my schoolmates later in life. Those who continued their studies, mainly because nobody knew where to send them back to, ended up in politics, or assimilated in the big cities. Others, most of them, spent their lives looking for their own identities and never found them.

"As for me, the announcement of my return home came unexpectedly, shortly before Christmas of the third or fourth year of patience. I have a crystal clear memory of Father Tyrone notifying me in a studied neutral tone that my parents had "requested" my return to Nogha Ti. The news floored me. I had seen them only on a couple of occasions since the day they left me with the missionaries. You see, they couldn't afford the luxury of travelling regularly to Yellowknife.

"Their first visit had lasted just a short while. We were in a waiting room at the school which I had never seen before. We sat on worn green velvet sofas; thick curtains of the same color allowed a heavy sunbeam loaded with dust specks through. We were silent, like strangers, not knowing what to say. We did not even smell the same anymore. I recognized their familiar scent of caribou hide and smoke that, as a small child, I had never remarked because I was within that scent, within that warm familiar circle. I reckon they also noticed my pungent smell of detergent and chalk. The distance was so intimidating that we never even dared to touch each other.

"The second visit was the next summer. It had been a good hunting year and my father took us to eat an ice cream at the Wild Cat Cafe. We ate it in silence, sitting around the table. My mother had a new baby on her back, my sister Adelle. Curiously, I did not feel jealous of her closeness to my mother, the smell of mother's milk and sweat that came from the warm hood filled with dry lichen where she slept so close to my mother's body. Maybe I had come to feel my mother was so faraway from me that I didn't even have the right to be jealous.

"At the Cafe and during the walk back to school, I noticed my mother darting furtive glances at me, at my body, scrutinizing me part by part, perhaps smelling me, perhaps resuscitating me from her book of the dead. But I would never have imagined they would want me back. I was no longer theirs, they were no longer mine. I thought that was clear for all of us. So, when Father Tyrone gave me the news, after the initial pang of euphoria about being wanted by them, I realized a thick curtain had been in front of my eyes for a long time and now it had suddenly fallen down and reality was there, in front of me, bare and frightening, like the teeth of a wolf. It was not only the fear of leaving Father Tyrone, but returning to my parents meant I would have to prove that I was all right, that I was useful, not a burden. That I could hunt and fish, lay a trap line, cut the meat, tan the hide. But the fact was I was not even sure I would be able to endure the cold, after so much time living in the suffocating heat of the white men's buildings. Did Father Tyrone understand this? Did he realize that life in the bush was already something remote and exotic to me, as a Jules Verne novel?

"'Your mom wants you to come back, Jimmy. She cannot wait to see you,' he said, rubbing the top of my head. I shrugged, ready to accept my destiny, but the priest seemed to be still full of explanations to deliver. 'I can do nothing about it, you know that, don't you?' He squatted down to look directly into my eyes, and then, in the sincere anguish of his stare, I understood that the situation was much more complicated than I knew. 'But you know what? You can take the books. All your favorites. New copies, not the ones you massacred miserably. And I will still fly to Nogha Ti and I will bring you new detective books and comics, cowboy novels... We will see each other and I will kick your butt at backgammon.'

"'Well, we'll see about that,' I said, forcing a smile. He stood up because he could not keep looking at me, and I spoke to the blackness of his cassock. 'Then, what was all the patience for?' I asked. He kneeled in front of me again, and this time, it was a man-to-man stare.

"'Because without the patience you would never have met *Huckleberry Finn*, or *Oliver Twist*, or *Captain Ahab*, or *Dick Tracy*. Your world is changing, Jimmy,' he said holding my shoulders tightly. 'For good or bad, your world is going to be forced to suffer in a few years a change that other countries have undergone in centuries. Thanks to your patience, you will understand this change better. You will find your way better. Like in a blizzard. I am very proud of you, Jimmy.' Then he stood up and left without saying goodbye, and I know he was crying because his spirit shook around him.

"One chilly January morning, at about fifty below, I said good-bye to Father Tyrone in the sober Yellowknife airport and, just as I had come to this strange place, I left it. I climbed the stairs to the airplane, this time without kicking and screaming, but not for the lack of panic. From the gate I turned around to watch the priest. His long dark silhouette shook in the insufficient coat and there was a strange mixture of restlessness and faith in his expression. In that moment, I thought I would never come back to that world of objects made by strangers, of barren patience and imposed gloom, of doggish obedience and sickening boredom, but also of passions, learning, and books. And more than anything, I had come to love that tall, dark priest.

"The excitement of flying eclipsed my fears for a while, but I'd say this made things worse, because upon landing, reality hit me brutally. The airplane landed in the main street and right there, where the craft stopped, almost buried in the snow raised by the skis, my parents and my sister Adele were waiting for me awkwardly. As soon as I came down, I tried to make eye contact with my sister, for I thought a child would be more approachable, but she was semi-hidden behind my mom, clutching her caribou skirt and she stared at me warily from there. After all I was a stranger for her. Her big brother who came from another world. My father's expression, hostile by nature, became even more somber as he saw my crutches. He obviously was expecting a full recovery, a miracle. However, to my amazement, he took two big strides and gave me a long tight hug I will never forget. I sunk my face in the fox collar of his jacket, inhaling greedily the familiar scent of smoke, sweat and pine needles, and tears unexpectedly welled up in my eyes. Big hot tears, the kind that wash away sadness held for a long time. Then my mother, also with tears in her eyes, touched me all over with hard exploring fingers, looking, smelling, trying to check that, to some extent, I was okay, in spite of the crutches, and that I would not die, leaving her soul scorched in horror and pain.

"Everything had changed in the village. Starting with its location. The village had been moved to the other side of the lake, following a change in the best fishing areas. There were still some tents, but most people lived in log cabins, like the white men. How could they hunt and trap in cabins that could not be moved was a mystery to me. There was also a church in construction, although not as big as the one I frequented in Yellowknife. I had expected to find my village just as it was in my memory, and this was shocking. Everything was shocking, but the worst thing was that I had forgotten my own language. I had not thought about this problem before and I started to understand the magnitude of it as we walked on the main street. People kept welcoming me back in town, patting my shoulder and head affectionately and laughing, delighted to witness my unlikely return. They asked me questions and provided advice I did not understand at all. I nodded, shielding myself in my weariness and shyness and feeling more and more isolated and lonely, as though I were inside one of those crystal balls full of snow. Lots and lots of snow.

"Gradually I got familiar with my language again, and was able to communicate with my people, but until I got there, life was quite hard for me. My father and I went out to hunt and set trap lines in the bush. I was supposed to learn these arts from him, but he did not understand my inexperienced questions and I did not understand his rough directions, on which our survival relied.

"I'll say in my favor that I was eager to learn. I've always been, but my traps hardly ever caught anything and my father picked them up empty with hardly concealed fury. Fact is, my focus was mainly on catching up to him on my crutches in the cold wilderness, without complaining, through the long hours, days and weeks that the hunting lasted. This endeavor took a superhuman effort of physical endurance. To me it was a triumph to be able to keep my tears inside as the cold stuck needles all over my body. Trying to suppress my agony did not leave much space for learning.

"Often I felt, with the sensitive spot we all have at the nape of our neck, which is like a third eye, my father watching me prepare the traps, or trying to cut the caribou on the snow fast enough to prevent it from freezing, making its meat and its death useless. He was gauging the swiftness, the strength and precision of my every move, with a slight uneasy frown, like an animal smelling his offspring. If I happened to turn to him, he was already looking somewhere else, engaged in some task or another, but still with that worried frown.

"They all expected me to help my father. To hunt and provide for the clan when he was old. This was my mission, and in a Dogrib community, back then, those who could not undertake their mission were labeled as burden. They were fed, but not eagerly, and they were given irrelevant tasks. They formed the group of weak beings that needed to be protected because they had not been blessed with the hunters' fate. Needless to say I did not want to be a part of that group and I turned away, scared and annoyed whenever one of them approached me. Speaking to them, it seemed to me back then, was like sinking slowly in their ghostly sad clan. Now, seen in perspective, from the age of understanding, I realize that those people were the only ones that were sympathetic to me and did not laugh at my predicaments. And I, stupid kid, always reciprocated their compassion with fear and anger.

"All my friends, the kids of my age, could already manage without a problem as hunters and fishermen and those who were twelve or thirteen were already looking for a mate to marry and have children. However, no mother allowed her daughter to return my stares, because they did not believe I could be a good provider. This was especially painful because I had the same fire in my body as the rest of the kids, the same longing for another body, for someone with whom I wouldn't need to feel so self-aware of my imperfection, and yet I feared I would spend the rest of my life alone, deprived of the company of women, those luminous beings that back then, were a mystery to me, and still are today.

"All of what I had learnt from the white men in Yellowknife was useless and incomprehensible among my people, where schooled kids could be counted with the fingers of one hand and most of the time were not in the community, but at the residential school back in Yellowknife. Speaking English, being able to handle figures, read or write did not help when it came to hunting, fishing or facing a hungry bear. Add my disability to the equation and you had a lonely isolated boy, far away from his mission or his dreams.

"The books that Father Tyrone had given me ended up being used as kindling by my father. I tried to hide them, because it comforted me to read them at the faint gas lamp light in the long winter nights at the cabin. They reminded me that the faraway world with warm rooms, comfortable beds and dainty ladies with little white hands that smelled of flowers still existed somewhere and I could perhaps go back there if things became uglier. Back to the world of boredom, of patience, but after all, that world was easy. I suspect that my father always felt offended by those books, which he could not read. So he kept burning them, trying to conceal how important it was for him to destruct them, to defeat them. I still kept some loose pages of my favorites under my mattress on the floor, reconstructing the whole stories, which I knew by heart, in my mind. Sometimes I even changed them, noticing how a subtle detail taken or added here or there gave the book a completely different ending. I anxiously awaited Father Tyrone's arrival, since he always brought me a book or a comic magazine, that I would hide with my stash and read hastily, before it, too, ended up in the stove.

"By the time I recovered my ability to communicate in Dogrib, there was already a big gap between me and the community. I had taken a jump by going to the white men's school and it was a jump with no return. I had the white man's stigma. I was not good in the tasks related to my role in life and I knew stuff that was incomprehensible and even intimidating for my peers. I was familiar with the swarm of little details that accompanied the white men, who were slowly but surely surrounding us. I knew about money, business, police, doctors, and alcohol. Even my father, with time, started to detach from me, not knowing whether to pity or fear me. He kept working on my training as a hunter, but he knew that I had gone through a very important change and it was beyond his capacity to correct it or to understand it.

"He was right. I was a pathetic hunter and trapper. For starters, most of the times I had to ride on the sled, otherwise I would slow us down unbearably on the snow. Then there was the temperature problem. In spite of my concentration and effort, I still could not tolerate the cold. My bones yearned for the comfortable, warm, gloomy rooms at the hospital. My mother made me a heavy beaver coat with the best pelts we—or rather my father—had got on the land. Pelts that would have bought us tea, sugar, flour, tobacco and ammunition for several months. My father stared at me, half amused half furious, and shouted, 'How the hell are you going to hunt dressed like that? You can hardly move in those furs. Have you ever seen a wolf hunt in a beaver coat? That's what you are, a wolf in a beaver coat', and he laughed loudly. With time, this became my shameful nickname. 'Wolf in a beaver coat.' 'Well,' I said to myself, resigned. 'At least they say wolf, not muskrat or chipmunk.'

"With time I reluctantly moved on from the tasks that were impossible in my physical condition and started to take on duties that were the provenance of women or the elderly. Duties like tanning the furs, cutting the meat and salting it, covering the tents' soil with branches over the snow, cutting wood. My father did not oppose this change because it was very useful to him to count on someone who was expert in these arts when we travelled, just the two of us, for several weeks. However, he never expressed his approval. I never stopped being the 'wolf in a beaver coat.'

"Only later, much later, when thanks to my education I was able to start the first grocery store in Nogha Ti, did he acknowledge me as a real man, able to provide for a family, but by then his recognition was not so important to me. During my childhood and teenage years, I needed it like drinking water. When it finally came I accepted it with resentment, with the cynical conviction that my worth had increased in his eyes when his own started to drop, when hunting had stopped being vital and one could buy a can of meat at my store. When people could no longer live on trapping because the white men had decided it was a cruelty to kill animals and the price of furs bottomed out. When the good hunters migrated to the dark depths of the mines. When he was faced with the terrible certainty that the skills he had transmitted to his children would not help them in the new world. The new world that, in accord with Father Tyrone's prophesy, was devouring us and most of all, when this changing world sunk our people in alcohol and disenchantment."

Jimmy let the memories dissolve in the peaceful darkness of his granddaughter's room. He was not telling the story to her, but he was taking her into the story, enveloping her in it, like in a dance in front of the fire, burning things that still hurt, reviving the scents and the textures, the varied sounds of so many winter days. His eyes of many years rested on his grandchild's closed eyes and that tired loving stare was more the story than the story itself, for it contained the story in the same way he had drank it in, sometimes in reluctant small sips, sometimes in big gulps.

He stood up and walked warily to the window to see the starry night, as if his son's death had a physical presence that, like a bear or a wolf, could sneak in stealthily, leaving bloody prints on the snow. The news. The certainty. The axe that was about to fall on his neck. He shut the curtains silently. That moment was just for the two of them, not for the spirits or the demons, or the neighbors.

V

The snowmobile's engine coughed again, this time a powerful bang, then it jerked violently and stopped. The vehicle slid sideways for about twenty yards, not too far, because the layer of snow piled on the track brought it to a smooth stop. Once the engine's roar was silenced, the blizzard's holler imposed its dreadful absolute presence as though it was coming from inside Amorak's own head. "Shit!" he shouted, punching the machine in anger.

He was dressed insufficiently for the cold and he was starting to feel pain in his fingers and toes. Worst of all was fear, that was giving his thoughts maddened bat wings. With the headlights off, darkness was total. Even after his eyes adapted to it, he could barely see, beyond the shell of his helmet, the snowflakes swarming him, as though hungry for his flesh. It would be useless to look for the red light that signaled salvation. "Paff, paff, paff", the unmistakable noise that could be perfectly heard in normal weather conditions. Impossible. That massive constant shriek filled everything. Everything.

Go to the bush, look for the shelter of the trees, said a weak voice, the voice of his mother, always thick with liquor. His first mother, that was. The weak helpless creature who had died in that sled, just like he was going to die now. But no. Who the hell was talking about dying? No one was dying. This was just a mechanical problem that would be solved and which he would tell his buddies about around the fire once he was back home.

He dismounted with self-imposed determination. I can make it. For sure I can. I must surely be half way by now and the refuge can't be far away. It must be right there. I can't be that lost. *Go into the bush and look for shelter there, make yourself a lean-to,* the little voice repeated in his ear and he could almost smell the alcohol inside his helmet. For some reason, this was not unpleasant at all. The bush. But, what if the bush is not enough, what if my snowsuit, my mitts, my boots, my helmet, are not enough? What if I die frozen, trapped in the bush, like a rabbit in a snare? What if the refuge is just a mile away and I stay here, frozen in the bush, a twenty minutes walk from salvation?

He crouched by the snowmobile to shelter from the wind while he considered his options. It was practically impossible to think clearly with the deafening scream of the storm in his ears. He opened the trunk and took out one of the bottles of whisky. He opened it, then raised his helmet's visor just enough to let the bottleneck in and took two big gulps. The liquor warmed up his throat, then his stomach. It gave him a brief moment of serenity. He took several more gulps. He needed to calm down. Calm down for real.

Perhaps the storm would subside soon, he thought, hopeful. Sometimes they lasted a couple of hours, sometimes a couple of days. It was impossible to know. Maybe it was wiser to wait for help… "Wait for what?" His mind shot back, this time in his father's voice. "For exposure and whisky to disable you and leave you to experience a painful death?" Amorak agreed with this viewpoint, but he had not been hunting or trapping on the land for very long. How could he build himself a lean-to? He had never made one in the middle of a blizzard. At least not alone. He did not have an axe or a blanket. Zero. Nada. He took another gulp from the bottle and drank greedily, trying to expel the cold from his body. As he stood up, he noticed the pleasant familiar dizziness in his head.

He staggered in the deep snow, leaning his body against the wind through the pitch-black night. Immediately he reached the lattice of spruce and brush that made an almost impenetrable wall. With snow up to his hips, he advanced into the bush, feeling his way blindly in search of a possible entry into the tight packed hedge of spruce and brush. It was not easy. He did not want to tear his snowsuit, since that would result in a sure death. He hit the branches with the bottle and tried to push himself in, but the tough frozen twigs kept him away implacably, as though he were trying to get under the skin of a live animal.

He stopped for a moment to catch his breath. Finally, after an angry push, he got himself into the brush, hardly half a meter. He heard the sound of his snowsuit fabric tearing and he swore again between his teeth. The push of the wind had suddenly stopped, but not the cold and the howling. With clumsy moves, he tried to make himself some room in the bushes and he curled up, ready to wait for the end of the storm. He was lucky to have the bottle, he thought, taking another pair of sips. How could he have taken off from Yellowknife, heading to Nogha Ti, one hundred and fifty kilometers in the middle of nowhere in a winter subarctic night, without foreseeing this could happen? Where was the instinct his native blood should have held? As soon as he was out of this blizzard, he had to ask some buddy to take him hunting in the bush, to get back in touch with nature. If he ever came out of this, that was.

The chill kept stabbing at his fingers and toes mercilessly and the pain was creeping up his legs, his knees, his hips, his elbows and shoulders. Then the certainty that he would die frozen if he stayed in that bush hit him like a punch on the face. He did not belong in the taiga and the taiga no longer welcomed him, did not recognize him as hers nor release her survival secrets to him, for he had discarded those secrets for years, considering them useless. It was like being in the arms of a woman who did not love him any more. He had the vision of the policemen rescuing his corpse from those frozen branches, bottle in the hand, like an idiot. Horrified, he stood up, with a determination bordering fury and made up his mind to try to make it to the refuge.

It was not difficult to get back to the snowmobile, which was by now covered in snow. He would just follow the track and probably he would soon see the red light, paff, paff, paff. It had to have been designed to be seen even in the blizzard, what the hell, wasn't *that* precisely the purpose of the damned thing?

He started to walk, trying to ignore the excruciating pain that extended through his whole body. At some fifty meters from the snowmobile, he took another couple of swigs, as medicine, he said to himself with a bitter smile. Then he reconsidered. Perhaps he should go back and take another bottle. This one was getting lighter by the moment. The liquor would keep him warm along the way. Would ease the pain in his limbs. He made his way back to the vehicle, wondering whether or not he was signing his own death sentence by doing this. This time it took him longer to find the snowmobile, probing the deep snow until his gloved hand touched the machine and his fingertips shot back a metallic thunder of pain that reached the back of his neck. He screamed and held his arm with his other hand, grinding his teeth, trying to contain his panic and agony.

He hunkered down by the side of the machine to fend off the wind. Panting, he dug through the snow to be able to open the trunk. His bottles were there. He tossed the half empty one on the snow and picked up two new ones. He could not see them, but he could picture in his mind their amber shine. That was all he had in that moment, his only support in this hostile dark tomb. Come to think of it, it was fair enough, wasn't it? He was going to die just as he had lived: alone with his whisky. He laughed an unmerry loud laughter that scared him as if it was not his own voice, but a malignant spirit celebrating his anguish, thirsty for his blood. "No, no, no, no, who's talking about death? No one's gonna die here today," he whispered to himself in reassurance, but his own soft voice sounded even weirder than the laughter. A macabre mockery. Better not to think. Pick up the bottle and start walking. You're five minutes from the refuge. It can't be any other way. The red light, paff, paff, paff. The firewood—for sure there must be dry firewood inside, and a fireplace or a stove to make a good fire, some bunk beds and a table. Coffee, tea, perhaps even some canned stew or dry caribou—and if there is none, bid deal, I have these, he thought, squeezing the two bottles in his hands, which sent another pang of pain through his arms.

He sat on the snow and reclined his back on the machine. Just a little break and he would continue the march. The rough voice, weaker and weaker inside him, urged him not to sit down to rest, but fatigue was stronger and the warmth of whisky was making him feel secure in the improvised shelter of the snowmobile. Just a moment. Couldn't the blizzard and the pain and the darkness give him just a moment to think? "Think about what?" asked the indignant small voice inside, "Think about quitting, that's what. Quitting is what you have always done and quitting is what you're doing now. There's no thinking, Amorak. There's walking or dying."

He knew this was true, but a fatigue stronger than himself made him heavy as lead. Just one moment, he thought, letting his eyelids drop and trying to bring back the memory of the warmth of his home in Nogha Ti. The yellowish light in the living room, the humming of the TV, the smell of coffee and stew.

When he came out of this reverie, he was back there, at home, there had never been a blizzard, just a bad hangoverish nightmare as he lay passed out on the sofa. Music hammered behind the closed door of his son's bedroom, the TV was, of course, on and there was the soft clattering of his wife and daughter laying the table for supper in the kitchen. Chicken. It was roasted chicken, his favorite. An un-earthly warmth enveloped his body and soul, a massive relief of salvation, a thankfulness that was beyond any joy he had ever experienced.

He observed his daughter through the open kitchen door, her moves that were delicate and powerful at the same time. He hated himself, as he did every time he looked at her because her forlorn beauty reflected the brutality of the harm he had inflicted on her. The harm that could never be repaired and had made him damned without absolution.

It was the darkness, he wanted to claim to himself. The darkness within him that made him hurt her, and the more he hated himself for doing it, the bigger his resentment and his desire to hurt her became. And a shame like that could only be washed out with booze. Gallons and gallons of booze.

He wondered how long he had felt like that, like he was already dead and nothing mattered anymore and dignity, love and peace were impossible.

The women were now making tea in the kitchen. The familiar whistling of the kettle joined the small noises in the house. He wanted to stand up and hug his daughter—as a father this time—and tell her that maybe happiness was still possible, that perhaps he could try to be a father. But when he tried, a mortal twinge of pain shook his whole body. The kettle's whistle rose up unnaturally. "Please, stop that fucking kettle, please!" he tried to scream, but no sound came out of his throat, not even air, and the whistle kept rising, getting into his head like an ice pick until it became the holler of the blizzard. He opened his eyes to the wall of snow in front of him and the stabbing pain, so intense it drew tears from his eyes.

He did not know for how long had he been sleeping, but he had to start off if he wanted to survive. Standing up took more strength than he thought he had, but he was relieved to notice that it was easier to walk. The wind was not pushing so hard. Perhaps the snowstorm was relenting. Yet the wolfish maddened howl of the wind was still inside his skull, poisoning him with pain and horror.

Now the snow radiated some eerie faint bluish luminescence. In spite of his disorientation, he knew the general direction he needed to walk in, for there was no other way, and every time he strayed he bumped into the dense bush and spruce wall. Pain was now taking over his every nerve, bone, muscle, every hair follicle. But he kept walking like a robot through the strange fluorescent snow that enveloped everything. By his sides, the bottles supported him, like crutches holding him to the world.

It was impossible to measure time or distance. The thing was just to go ahead. Perhaps the screaming would quiet down. Perhaps the snow would settle and give him a chance to survive. One foot, then the other, one foot, then the other. That was all he needed to think about. Forget the pain, forget the red hot needles that seemed to cover his body. But how could he, when the pain was so massive that it had seized him, that it had become him.

He was about to give in when, against all odds, he saw the red light high up above the black and white mass of the forest. You could hardly see it through the blizzard, but there it was, not far away, probably some two hundred yards. He sped up, laughing like a madman.

VI

Jimmy considered going out for a smoke, but he did not have much time, not to mention that in order to exit the house, he needed to pass by his daughter in law and her stabbing stare. He'd rather not, he thought with a snort. To defeat anxiety, he took a cigarette out of the package and tapped it in his fingers. He put it in his lips without lighting up and kept on with his story.

"One day—one of those first glorious days of last early spring— as I'm cutting wood by my house, the SAO's wife, you know, that foreign young lady that is always horrified by the weather, she stops to have a chat with me." Jimmy laughed fondly. "She's back from the store, loaded with plastic bags that must be cutting her fingers something bad. She greets me with a nod, which I return, but seeing as she stops, I reckon she's in the mood for a chat. I could use a rest and a smoke, so I leave the axe by the door and I walk to meet her at the path. Of course I don't invite her in, because I am alone at home and it would be inappropriate for two married adults to meet like that. Anyway, it is not cold, must be fifteen below and the sun is shining on a blue cloudless sky, so an outdoor chat will be pleasant, I think.

"Then I notice how much I was needing a break, since it takes me a while to stop panting and my face is burning with heat. I have to take care of myself. My seventy eight winters, plus some extra pounds, the ugly smoking habit and a couple of whiskies every now and then have earned my heart the label *clockwork bomb*, granted by my doctor, the one who wants me to live forever. But

I wonder, aren't all hearts clockwork bombs, ticking their way towards the grave?

"'How's it going?' I ask, wheezing, as she offers me a hand crossed by plastic bags marks, which I shake.

"'Good,' she answers. She looks uneasy, as though she has something in mind she wants to say but she can't find the right way. She looks around, as if the trees or the neighbors' houses could provide the right formula.

"'Spring seems to have settled in, eh? At least what you people call spring.' We both laugh at that thought.

"'I guess,' she goes on, 'the bears will soon wake up from hibernation.' Her face is a mixture of horror and fascination that is one of the most attractive features of white women. I shake my head.

"'Not yet. Not with this weather they won't. Giv'em at least one more month,' I answer.

"'Jimmy, what do you have to do if you come across a bear?' She asks. 'I know running is useless. Then there are people who say you should make a lot of noise and others who say the noise will piss the bear off and make things worse. I've heard some people say you must play dead, lying face down so that they don't tear up your stomach to eat what's inside. But I've also heard that Dogrib People have a secret formula that you whisper to the bear to deter an attack. Is that so?'

"I laugh out loud. 'You whites are always looking for what to do when faced with any situation, and if there is nothing you can do, you feel stupid or horrified. Or impotent. As if one had the control over any situations in life.'

"She stares at me confused, so I explain. 'If you come across a bear, you don't have control. The bear does. Unless you have a shotgun and ironclad hunter nerves, but I guess that's not your case, so, what can you do? As you very well said, you'd never outrun a bear and if you scream you have an equal chance of scaring him or prompting an attack. If you come across a bear, you don't decide: he does. You don't need to do anything.'

"The woman crosses her arms, as if defending herself from my explanation, for there is nothing worse to tell a white person than he or she can do nothing when faced with a life threatening situation. She realizes I am amused at her attitude and she uncrosses her arms, laughing.

"'Yeah, but what about the Dogrib magical words. Are they for real?'

"This woman makes me laugh again. She's not ready to give in. She wants her control back. 'They are not magical,' I say. 'But Dogrib and Bear have shared this land in harmony for ages and it can be said we understand each other. What we actually say to the bear is, *I am not food. If you kill me, my people will come to kill you and your cubs. They will follow your tracks and kill you. This is unavoidable because it is in human nature. Perhaps now you are hungry because you have just awakened from the long sleep, with your fur stuck to your bones. But soon the ice will melt and you will catch good fish and there will be berries in the bush. You will get fat and lustrous. Wouldn't it be a shame that both of us had to die? Follow your way and I will follow mine. This is basically what you say to the bear, but ultimately it is the bear who decides.'*

"I take out my cigarette package from my shirt's pocket and I offer her one, which she politely refuses. I light up mine. I like this woman because she actually listens. She sinks into the story like water into a cloth. So I go on. 'And yet this would be good only for the sah, the black bear, that normally tries to stay away from men, unless he's starving or protecting a cub. The sah cho, the grizzly bear and the Kodiak bear are a different story. Further beyond, where the trees are higher is where the friggin' beasts live,' I say, and suddenly my mind flies to a memory accurate and sharp like the smell of blood. Now I know I will have to tell the whole story, because we are together in the story and my senses are bringing it back, no matter how painful and dreadful it feels.

"'Those bears eat people. They are men hunters. They can track you for days if needed. For the sah-cho we are food, so it would make no sense to try to tell him otherwise. But don't worry, those don't come around here,' I clarify when I see her horrified expression. 'When I was twelve, I had the chance to see one close up. Close enough to feel its power and its anger.'

"That year, my father and I went to spend the winter close to Tsiigehtchik, way up in the Northwest, where they had told us a good hunter could get good furs: martens, wolves, muskrat, beaver and whatnot. All the stuff the Bay paid big bucks for at that time. It took us a month to get there in our dogsled, but it was worth it. We got a lot of furs and we sold them for a lot of money. Hell, we had actual white money, somba.' I chuckle and a liquid compulsive cough invades me. Maybe I do have to slow down on the cigarettes. Perhaps next Christmas.

"Although I do not tell the white woman about it, this travel, Jiewa, was my father's ultimate test of my survival abilities. He was determining whether I would be of any use in life or if I deserved to die or be abandoned in one of the missions to disappear in the nothingness. This was an initiation journey in which the rest of my life was being decided and I was conscious of it every minute, in every snare I prepared, in every fire I built.

"'During our stay in Tsiigehtchik,' I continue for the white woman, 'my father was in a relationship with a young Gwitchin woman. I don't remember her name. She was round and small, smiling and silent, with slanted serene eyes. She couldn't have been more than sixteen and she was very beautiful; my dad was besotted, and he kept delaying our return. I kept warning him about the onset of the early spring. During that time of year travelling became very dangerous and painstaking, with the dogs' paws always sunk in sludge; crossing the many frozen lakes became slow and exhausting, since you practically had to pull the dogs across the surface while searching for holes. The rivers we normally used as roads became unstable and at any moment the thin ice crust could break swallowing men, sleds and dogs. In my frustration I saw the days grow longer and the snow wetter, like my father's heart.' I shake my head at the memory and spit on the snow to take it off my mind. 'For sure the girl was very pretty,' I admit, inhaling deeply into my cigarette and squinting at the ghost of her image in the smoke. 'Much prettier than my mom, indeed. But then she hadn't borne four children and lost one.'

"'The fact is my father spent his days in a placid idleness and he disappeared every night to sleep with the girl, leaving me alone in the tent. I covered my head with the blanket so I wouldn't hear the wolves' howling, but what really scared me was the thought that one morning he might not return. That he might stay with the woman for ever and abandon me in that place, from where I would never be able to get back to my family especially with early spring spreading all over the foreign land.

"'So, one dawn, when he was coming back from his romance night, I confronted him. I said, 'Father, either we return now or we will not be able to move until the next winter.' He stared at me for some seconds, with fire in his eyes, then he slapped me out of his way, entered into the tent, and fell asleep. When he woke up in the early afternoon, I had already packed everything and we were set up to go. I had checked and packed the snares and traps, and all our supplies, tools and guns were neatly wrapped in blankets and tied up in the sled.

"'He didn't say a word. He just folded the tent, hooked the dogs and we finally headed towards home. As I had foreseen, it was tough going and probably we should not have started the journey. We advanced slowly and had to bandage the dogs' paws every night. My dad was gloomy and silent and I chose to stay quiet, so as not to provoke him. We covered miles and miles of forest in silence, sharing the work on the way, which became tougher as the weather kept improving. We had to cross dozens of small lakes and ponds, with our mukluks soaking in sludge and we had to stop every now and then and light a fire to dry our clothes. We hunted rabbit, beaver, or whatever was at hand to eat and feed the starving dogs. Sometimes, when the weather was warm, we camped for one day to tend to the dogs' and our own ice wounds. We laid some snares, lit a good fire and extended our stay to regain our strength.

"'It was one of those days, with an intensely blue sky and not a breeze in the trees, that we came across it. We had just started off and were walking slowly through a pine forest. My dad sang an old song between his teeth, which was a good sign that he was starting to forget the Gwitchin girl. Then he stopped his humming as suddenly as if his throat had been clogged. He stopped the dogs, took a couple of cautious steps and stood there, still, tense like a drum, looking among the branches at a point I could not see.

"'He took off his mitt and extended his bare right hand to me and I handed him his shotgun. As he raised it, I followed the barrels' direction and then I saw it. Even though we were far away, on a small hill at the other side of a ravine, its size and its presence were overpowering. We had never seen anything like that. We watched him in awe for a while. He seemed to be playing, scratching his back with a tree bark, or rolling lazily in the dirty snow. My father lowered the shotgun and gave it back to me. It was not close enough. We saw the sah-cho disappear leaping playfully into the bush.

"'What's he playing?' I whispered, putting the shotgun back on the sled.

"'He doesn't play,' my father answered shaking his head, his gaze still fixed on the place where the bear had disappeared. 'He woke up too early from the big sleep. He can't fish because the water is frozen. There's no berries. He's starved. The breeze blows toward him and he's pretending not to notice us. He's hunting us, Jimmy, that's what he does. He wants us to come closer.'

"'My father was a brute, but he had an inborn wisdom when it came to understanding animal behavior. 'Seeing a bear out of season is a bad sign,' I said, trying hopelessly to change what I already knew my father's decision would be. 'We're going to hunt this bear,' he said, ignoring my comment and confirming my fear. 'Take the sled to that clearing overlooking the ravine,' he said, pointing at a small clearing, at about three hundred yards. 'Set the tent up there and wait for me. I'm going to follow him. He's bound to have left tracks in all this sludge.' He took the shotgun and his ammunition and disappeared in the bush.

"'I steered the sled towards the point he had indicated with a cold feeling that there was something askew in the picture, I wouldn't know how to explain it. As if you found a fish in the stomach of a caribou. But I knew my father had also noticed and if he wanted to go ahead with the game, there was nothing I could say or do.

"'As I followed the ridge of the ravine, I heard the skis hissing over the snow and something was wrong with this because it was the only sound one could hear. A deep silence had closed around us like a curse. Even the dogs were silent, but they walked stiffly, the hairs on their backs standing like porcupine quills. We all knew the bear was following us. Up close, too. And we had fallen into his trap like rabbits, but it was too late to do anything about it and we walked in a dead silence, as though we were in a pass that had an avalanche risk. Any word, any rough move, might hasten our imminent death. All my senses screamed in my head and an electric feeling tickled my skull. Don't turn around, don't turn around, was all I could repeat to myself in my frenzied mind. He was there, right there. Will I have time to get my shotgun? The question burned inside my mind. Was it loaded? Was it? It always is. Why shouldn't it be now? Yeah, but you have been hunting for breakfast.

"'Cold sweat dripped along my spine and my forehead and my eyes felt itchy. Blood pounded in my ears so loudly I was sure the bear and the dogs could hear my fear. I was prey. I have been in danger in other occasions throughout my life, but there is nothing compared to the feeling of being the prey of a stalking predator.

"'I wondered where my father would be. Probably starting to read the tracks on the other side of the ravine. Then all of a sudden some branches shook on my left and then nothing mattered anymore. Not whether the shotgun was loaded or not, not whether I would have the time to take it and shoot. I was frozen, paralyzed in fear, awaiting the end. Fortunately, when the bush opened it was my father who came through it. *Nothing*, he said, *it looks as if the earth swallowed him*, he said trying to sound casual, but his tone told me he could also feel the animal and he was speaking loud to shake his own fear away. And it worked. It was as though the sah-cho had decided to grant us a truce as a part of the game.

"'We advanced to the small clearing my father had chosen and we set up camp as the daylight slipped away into an orange thick twilight. I lit a fire, but there was nothing to cook and I did not feel like going into the dark to get us supper, and fortunately my father didn't ask me to, so we ate dry meat without exchanging a single word, throwing wary glances at the exasperating silence of the dark forest. *Tomorrow we will be on our way*, my father said, throwing his last piece of meat to the dogs. *You were right. This bear is bad news.* He stood up, shaking the snow from his jacket and he entered the tent.'

"I finish my cigarette, holding it between my index and my thumb and I throw it in the snow with a grimace at a kind of fear that will remain in my bones for a lifetime. The white woman listens to my story without a blink.

"'Entering the tent was a mistake and we both knew it,' I continue. 'A simple structure of branches and canvas can never protect you from a bear. On the contrary, it boxes you in and leaves you without freedom of movement. On the other hand, that bear, precisely *that* bear was not going to relinquish his prey and he was probably just waiting for the fire to be extinguished before he attacked. The hunting had begun and it would only end with blood. This we knew. Why my father, an accomplished hunter, decided to wait for the beast in the tent is still a mystery to me. Perhaps that sah-cho awoke fears in him that were alien to his makeup. I think he felt the bear was hunting not only for his flesh, but for his very soul, and he was too scared to confront his ghosts, hidden in the blackness that surrounded us for miles and miles. So he stuck his head in the ground, like they say ostriches do when they feel threatened.

"'I laid on a fur mattress with my shotgun in my hands, waiting for the moment. My father sat on the opposite side of the tent, his shotgun over his crossed legs, rolling one cigarette after another with unnerving calm. He had not finished smoking the last one when a sudden blast of howling and grunting came from outside. By the time we could stand up, the beast had already attacked the dogs fiercely and killed three of them. It all happened so fast that we did not have time to react when the animal swerved and bit my father's shoulder with his massive jaws, making him scream in agony. I tried to aim the shotgun, but panic made me stumble and I fell over the tent that trapped me like a spider web. When I stood up I looked for my father in the howling and screaming fracas. The bear, which was closer than I had thought, so close I could touch his fur, was shaking my father like a ragdoll as he tossed the dogs into the bush with powerful blows.

"'For a second he stopped and stared at me, his eyes filled with a deadly fury. I have never seen anything so dreadful. He let go of my father and turned to me with a thundering roar, showing his lethal fangs and his black gums.

"'I heard a gunshot but was too stunned to realize it had come from my own weapon. I shot from stupor, without looking, without aiming, almost as a coincidence. I might as well have hit my father. But I was lucky and I hit the bear. I saw him run away hobbling through the bush. I was amazed at my own luck, then I heard my father mumbling something and I rushed to help him. He sat up painfully and looked around him. Four dead dogs, the sled and the tent in shambles, the smell of blood, the dogs' and his own, pervading the darkness. In how many seconds had that happened? None of us could tell. Time didn't matter anymore. We found the other four dogs, but one of them was deadly wounded and we had to kill it. My dad had very deep injuries in his shoulder and chest and I had also received, without noticing, a slight blow on my arm.

'As we slowly shook the nightmare away, we packed up and made our way back to Tsiigchtchik that very night, lest the bear, wounded and all, decided to come back for his prey. I feared my father might not make it there alive, for he was very seriously injured, but he always had a wolf's strength and he survived the attack. By the time we arrived in Tsiigehtchik, his wounds were almost cured and he was really pleased to reunite with his lover.'"

"'So, in the end you never made it to Nogha Ti that spring,' the white woman says. 'Never did,' I agree. 'Then by the fall, the girl ended up having my father's daughter and we had to rush out of the place, because the mom's parents were adamant on them getting married, even though my father had already explained he had wife and children in Nogha Ti and had provided for them abundantly in compensation. But the mom's father was an older man with a limp in his left leg and still four kids to feed plus now a granddaughter. He knew that my father was a good hunter and he wanted him in his clan by all means. When we left, he cursed us. He said that the same bear would come back to kill us. This curse unnerved my father, made his fear of the bear more present, so we took off in the middle of the winter, in order not to risk another encounter. Even so, throughout our long journey, he often stopped looking around warily, touching his chest and his shoulder as he did so, as though it were in his scars where he could feel the proximity of the beast. He believed that, since he had not killed the bear, it would follow him for the rest of his days like a deadly shade. And so he believed until the day he died from old age. With his dying breath he whispered, horrified, that he could see the bear coming to take him to the afterlife.

"'And what happened to your sister? Have you ever met her or had news from her?' the woman asked.

"'No, never. We had no news because we were far away and our families were not related, apart from the baby, of course. Besides, since my father did not want my mother to know about his love affair, we could not ask the people coming from up North to give us any information. But my father never forgot that Gwitchin woman.' As I tell the woman the story, my eyes pursue a ghost through her, where I still seem to see my sister at the other side of the barren lands, at the other side of time, life and death.

"'Often, when he sat down to drink at the kitchen table, his misty gaze got lost far away, as though thinking, *What if I had stayed, eh? If I had stayed with her? What then?* And his powerful hunter body seemed overthrown, defeated, from his grey head and tanned face, to the heavy boots. Then he shivered thinking of the bear and unconsciously he moved his hand to the scar on his chest. That terrible memory would always accompany the sweet reminiscence of the woman who I believe was the love of his life.

And that was the way in which the sah-cho exacted revenge on my father.'

"I light another cigarette to blow away the heavy parts of the story, like how my father never thanked me for saving his life, but rather blamed me for letting the bear escape wounded so he could curse us. Somehow I passed the initiation journey test. I was useful. I could hunt, I could trap, I could guide the dogs. Hell, I even saved my father's life. But I would never be worthy of his pride because I never gave the dead bear to him. My dignity as a hunter had been decided in the trajectory of that single bullet. But I don't say this to the white woman. This hurts too much. It even hurts now that I'm telling you.

"Anyhow, the woman thanks me for the story, which has clearly impressed her, and holds her plastic bags, ready to go. In her movements I notice she is pregnant. Not much, but she is. Perhaps even she doesn't know it yet, because it is her first. She says goodbye with a smile and as I watch her leave, ruminating on my heavy words, a pang of tenderness fills me. She looks so helpless and exotic in this place, with her sparkly warm weather gaze. Like a hallucination. With a new spasm of cough, I go back to my axe and my firewood and promise myself to smoke less."

VII

There it was, right in front of him. The red light, like the flashing of a ghostly beacon way up in the snowstorm, blinking at him over the dark bulky shape of the cabin. He could not hear its small cracking noise, lost in the wind's roar, but its red sharpness could cut through the snowflakes.

He stared at it for a moment, to let the vision sink in. Then he ran as fast as his pained legs allowed and pushed his way to the entrance. He had to dig for a while until he could open the door and when he finally did, he rushed inside and shut it behind him, resting his tired body against it for a while, wheezing, waiting for his limbs to feel alive again. He removed his mitts with the same care a surgeon would use to remove a bandage. His fingers ached so much he could hardly move them. He probed around in the darkness, careful not to bump his tender hands and soon he found a gas lamp and a box of matches on the windowsill. After several shaky attempts he lit the lamp and he contemplated in grateful wonder the miracle of the wooden room around him. A gush of inner warmth and thankfulness swept through him.

The cabin was just a rectangular space. In the opposite end to the door there were four empty bunk beds with rolled mattresses and blankets on them. In the centre there was a sturdy wooden table with four chairs. On the right side of the door, a stone fireplace with dry wood on both sides and right by the left side of the door there was a small gas stove on a counter with a kettle and on top of it, an alcove with some tins of ham and beans, tea and coffee.

Amorak left the lamp and the bottles on the table. He sat carefully on a chair and began to sob like a child. After some minutes, when he felt calmer, he took on the task of lighting a fire, which was not easy with his purple achy fingers, but at last he got a stable flame and he dragged his chair close to the fireplace, exhausted. Cold had seeped so deeply into his bones that he barely felt the fire's heat.

So it looks like I'm not dying from this one. He smiled, moving closer to the flames. When his eyes grew used to the dimness of the room, he inspected the walls of the cabin around him. They were bare except for some shelves and an old photograph on the wall, hardly visible in the dance of the fire and the gas lamp. It was one of these sepia tinted old pictures of an elder in the early Twentieth Century, probably one of the first elders who had initiated the treaties with the government of the white men. His face was hardened by the wind, his slanted eyes sparkled with intelligence and he was wearing a black hat way too big for his narrow head. He seemed to be looking at Amorak from the wall with a special intensity, as if he was there for him, as if he had something special to tell him. Nothing too kind, judging by the expression on his face.

Everything in the old man's faint image spoke of the important fights he had fought and the historical milestones he had accomplished in his life whilst all Amorak had done in his life was drink and work in order to drink some more. The intense blackness in the old man's eyes was bothering him. He stood up and hobbled over to the picture, to throw it in the fire, or just turn it around so that it could no longer bother him. But the frame was firmly nailed to the log wall, probably to keep it from being stolen.

Amorak laughed between his teeth as he took a blanket from one of the bunk beds and made his way back to the chair. Who was going to take away that ugly old man's picture? Then again, the frame could be used for something else. He sat at the table and drank from his bottle. The old man stared at him from the wall, his gaze impossible to ignore. Amorak confronted him as he played with the bottle in his hand.

"That's how it is, ol' man," he shouted. "That's what I am. It bothers you? Expected something better? What important thing did you do that allows you to judge me? Oh, yeah, you probably were in very important meetings with very important people that came from the South, bought some furs at a tenth of their price, hunted a couple of caribou, or even a bear, and back home, put your picture among their trophies. Right between the moose and the bear." He raised both hands to the wall without letting go of the bottle.

"Where did your important negotiations get you? Where did they get us? Look, ol' man," he screamed, spreading his arms like wings. "A bunch of Indians without roots and without future. We have lost everything. This used to be our land. Now we pay rent to live here. We get the worst jobs, the worst salaries. All we have left is booze. That's how it is," he said gulping loudly, defiantly, while he laughed. He coughed and the tang of blood filled his mouth. When he looked up again, the elder seemed even more infuriated. His expression was somber and intimidating. He squirmed uneasily on his chair and wrapped the blanket more tightly around his shoulders. Why couldn't the wind shut up? For how long did he have to stay there? If only pain could give him a truce, just to relax his muscles that were stiff as wood.

"And we can still be thankful, ol' man," he continued. "When the mining companies are through depleting our land, how are our communities going to be sustained? We don't hunt anymore. We don't fish. We must be thankful for these shitty jobs." A burst of laughter made him feel as if he had iron shavings in his throat and pain made in fold over his waist. When he raised his head, tears ran down his face. "That's what we have, ol' man. That's what we have. The time of warriors is over. The time of tribes is over. The time of clans is over. Each man pulls his own sled as best as he can. And it ain't easy, ol' man. It wasn't easy for you, but it ain't easy for me, so don't give me that look."

But the old man's face was actually changing. Or maybe he was losing his mind. The sparkling eyes came alive and an insane cruel blackness steamed up from a face that some moments ago only inspired dignity and respect. He covered his face with both hands and rubbed his eyes. Then he stood up and went to the stove to make himself some tea. Something warm in his stomach would help him relax. He stood by the kettle, his arms crossed, watching the blue dance of the gas fire, but always feeling the old man's stormy stare on the cold point in the nape of his neck.

The kettle's whistle startled him awake at his own kitchen in Nogha Ti. He still had the bottle in his hand but that was hardly new. What the hell was going on in his head?

He sat by the familiar green Formica table under the strong kitchen light, but the refuge's chipped pewter mug was still in his hand, full of hot tea. Every detail in his home kitchen presented itself with supernatural precision. He drummed his fingers on the table. They did not seem to hurt now. His daughter came and sat beside him. The ugly white kitchen light did not make her uglier. Quite on the contrary. He looked at her admiringly. He had never noticed how beautiful she was, but then again, had he ever looked deep in her soul?

His memories as a father mixed sickeningly with the other ones, the ones he could not name or bear to summon, the images that showed someone that looked like him assaulting his daughter without pleasure or happiness. But it could not be him. How could it be him?

And there she was, right in front of him. A black-haired teenage Dogrib with proud gaze and open curves, ready for life, so beautiful that it hurt to look at her. His daughter. But instead of slouching and biting her fingernails and hiding her face in her dirty hair curtain, as she used to, she walked now defiantly, with an aura of power and serenity. Perhaps she was the Jiewa that might have been, had it not been for him, her father. Did he still have the right to feel proud of her? No. He thought that feeling proud of her would be totally inappropriate. He had lost the right to feel proud of anything the first time he abused her and that was many years ago.

Now there was a wall between them. A wall of ice or crystal. He could not touch her or soil her anymore and he knew that if he even dared to try, the emptiness would return his own broken voice and this scared him more than death. She did not seem to see him either and it was all right like that. He thought he liked this renewed version of his daughter because it did not return his own ugliness. However, he thought, wouldn't it have been fantastic to be able to make her like that?

Too late, he said to himself bitterly. Yes, he had reached the refuge and was saved, but his daughter could not be saved. Or could she? Even then, it was sadly beautiful to contemplate this unlikely version of Jiewa, as harmonious and happy as she would never be.

He remembered her walking by the police station street, up and down, up and down. In the winter, at forty below, and in the summer, when the passing trucks covered her hair with dust. Sometimes she walked with her little brother in her arms, like a little mommy. Sometimes they walked together slowly in silence, like orphaned survivors of a catastrophe. Never until then had he wondered why they walked along the police station street. Now, as he watched from behind that cruel "too late" wall, he realized it was not a walk, but rather an exodus. They were not walking, but escaping from a home that should have been their safe haven but it was a place of tears and despair instead.

He shut his eyes tightly to escape that vision and then in the darkness of his eyelids, he could see the elder in the picture, his black stare nailed on him, on his spirit, this time loaded with a fiendish hatred, as if the blizzard's scream emerged from his very eyes. But the vision and the scream only lasted the fraction of an eternal second and his daughter was again in front of him. This time it was the real Jiewa, the one that slouched and bit her fingernails until they bled. He tried to read into her eyes and he only found fear. Fear of the moment when his dad would arrive from the mine with the pocket full of money and the trunk loaded with bootlegged booze, which he was supposed to sell in the village at four times its price, but which he normally drank himself.

Mom pitifully begged for some of the money for groceries and clothes before it all went to poker, but she hardly ever got milk, bread, flour and eggs. He said, laughing, that they did not need the money, for they could take free meat from the common storage hut where hunters left the cut of caribou to put it at the disposal of the community. And that was what they ate in the house: caribou stew, dry caribou, caribou roast, and dry fish. No fruit, no veggies, of course no candies. It was grandma who took care of their clothes, visiting relatives for hand-me-downs for her and her brother, and even sometimes bringing the occasional new garments.

What the hell, didn't he deserve some fun after two weeks working twelve hour shifts at the mine? Discussing this point always ended up in violence, so nobody dared to differ. A little bit of fun... If it had been fun at all.

He retraced his routines in his mind, like a man who has lost a valuable object. First thing he did when he arrived in his home was to lock the main door. He took off his snowsuit and his boots. He took out the bottles from the bags and lined them in the living room table. He liked to do this. It gave him a feeling of wealth, of bounty. His own collection of trophies. Some were amber, some green. Some were really beautiful with rounded shapes and shiny colors. Others were transparent. More transparent than water. More transparent than wind. His son Edzo had asked him once, in amazement, how could a man get drunk on something so transparent. He had laughed at the question and answered, "Don't worry, Edzo. Some day you'll know."

He liked to have the first five or six drinks alone. *To shake off the cold*, he said. He sat in front of the table, where the rainbow of bottles waited full of promise and he opened them one by one, removing the seals in silence, almost with reverence. Then he filled his glass again and again, "gloom, gloom, gloom, gloom," the liquid seemed to sing in mockery as it poured out of the bottles in the silence of the house.

Later on, when alcohol was already blurring the shapes and the reality around him, he called some friends, always the same ones, to share his drinks. They came as fast as ravens to a caribou carcass. One by one, the same well known faces sat around the table and they all knew for what purpose. No explanations or greetings were needed. No social excuses. They knew each other.

Sometimes they played cards, but mostly they drank and they did not stop until all the bottles were empty. Then they drank the ones the visitors had brought hidden in the sleeves of their parkas. This routine sometimes lasted several days and at the end of it, when the drinkers said goodbye feeling sick, broke and wasted, reality again drew its sharp edges around Amorak and the hangoverish rage took him over. Then he looked for his wife or his children, whoever was more handy, to download the anger on them and afterwards, when all he wanted was to give his soul to the devil, he looked for Jiewa.

He seldom found her these days, for she was strolling up and down the police station street, day and night. Maybe she dreamed of finding the courage to enter the square building and set her family free from her father. But she also knew that her people, including her own family, would never forgive her for delivering him to the police. She had seen it in other houses. Police were not their people. They were strangers and nobody wanted them sniffing their private problems. Any abuse report to them was regarded as a betrayal to the community and people who violated this unwritten law were isolated and ostracized.

But Jiewa dreamed that maybe one day one of the cops would notice her walking and wonder why those small kids were always prowling around. Perhaps a native cop, one who understood. A good man who would care to help them. Or even better, one of the women cops with whom she could talk friend to friend and let her long contained tears flood freely. But no. There was never such a cop. The cops were inside and she and her little brother were outside, and nobody ever noticed her. She was transparent like the lake water. Like the transparent liquor.

The problem was that mom also drank. She drank alone in the kitchen. Every now and then she stealthily approached the living room table as a spectral presence and refilled her glass to the rim, so that she would not have to return too soon. Then she took it to the kitchen, she sat by the window that looked on the lakeshore and she drank, her gaze lost somewhere very remote and very soft, where thoughts did not exist. If she didn't drink, everything would have been different. They could have gone together to some friends' or relatives' home while dad's binge lasted. But since she was at it as well, Jiewa could not stay at anybody's house without embarrassing her. So she just walked up and down, always with her little brother, because she did not want him to suffer the same things that she had and, even though she was just a little girl, she already had the dark certainty that it could happen to him too. They walked until the guests started to leave the house, which meant the booze was gone. Their parents would have passed out and that was the best moment to come back in quietly through the back door, their little faces stuck to the windows, spying the activity within the house, their ears alert and all their nerves standing. Only when the silence was total, they would open the door carefully, snatch a piece of bread from the pantry and go up to their bedrooms on their tippy-toes, to lock themselves, wrap their numb bodies into blankets and chew greedily the first food in a couple of days. They would remain locked there until the smell of coffee told them they could go out and expect some reasonable peace.

On one occasion, Edzo violated this curfew to go for a pee and came across his father on the landing. The frightened animal face on his son awoke the worst in Amorak's rage.

"What the hell are you staring at?" he asked with dangerous hostility. The kid did not answer, just shrank into a ball, ready to take the beating that was obviously coming.

"Answer me!" Amorak roared, although he did not really know what answer did he want. Just anger had taken over. Edzo peed his pants in terror and this enraged his father even more. He shot him the first kick that bumped his little body against the wall. Edzo opened his mouth to scream but no sound came out of it, and there were no tears from his wide open eyes.

The punching started with murderous intensity and he might have killed his own son for no reason, had not it been for Jiewa, who bravely opened her bedroom door and called Edzo with a womanly authority that left Amorak astonished for some seconds. Edzo escaped from his father's grip and rushed into his sister's bedroom. There he cried as Jiewa cradled him and sung to him softly, softly, almost in whispers. Then she healed his wounds and they cuddled together in bed, where they stayed for almost two days.

She was more Edzo's mom than his real mom. She made him meals and washed him when mom remained in bed for days, either passed out drunk or with her body covered in bruises. She played with Edzo and made him feel that sometimes they were at home, that laughter and warmth were possible.

However, her premature maturity had made her understand the true nature of what her father was doing with her body and a dark veil had fallen in front of her eyes. Other than Edzo, she hardly ever played or talked to any other children. She grew overweight and she had a strong body odor from not showering regularly, since she wanted nothing to do with her femininity. She only went to school every now and then, mostly to stay warm when there was no fuel or firewood in their house. Other than that, she attended just enough for the teachers not to be probing or phoning, or what was even worse, dropping by. If they got into their family's business, she would be in big trouble. So she stayed in the last row for the duration of the lessons, without interrupting, trying to be as inconspicuous as possible, not participating. Not participating had recently become her motto.

On her way back home, she used to stop at her grandpa's store. Grandpa and grandma were her only connection with the world of the living. Sometimes he made her sit at the cash register for a while, as an excuse to give her some money. She liked to sit there, protected by the machine, feeling important and distant as she tended to people and answered their small talk with monosyllables. In her grandpa's store she was in a real, safe and predictable world that was somehow hers.

But most of the time, Jiewa just expected the world to leave her alone. For childhood and teenage years to scurry away with their danger and pain. She envied her seventeen year old sister, who had two children and lived in Yellowknife. She longed for the anonymity of the city, where one could blend, like a stream into a river, become a little bit invisible, breath an impersonal air that was not polluted by ghosts.

Amorak sighed longingly, thinking of his girl when she was a girl—when he let her be a girl—chubby giggling Jiewa who dreamed big, sat on the floor and made beautiful multicolored pictures where she could fly. Back when she liked to watch Forrest Gump and eat bologna sandwiches.

His watery gaze could not be raised from the green Formica. The images were too heavy and his conscience was flickering like a flawed light bulb. Pain seemed to be appeasing, giving way to a general numbness. Numbness was better than pain, so he let it overwhelm him, almost gratefully.

"Why are you crying, dad?" Jiewa asked with motherly tenderness, but with a metallic coldness in her black eyes. Now she could see him, and she glided smoothly toward him, as though floating. "As if you were hearing this story for the first time… Poor dad…" she crooned as she passed by his face a hand that was colder than ice, colder than blizzard, colder than death. And he stayed there, frozen to his chair. He couldn't move and he couldn't talk. He would like to say so many things, but his throat was closed. His tongue, he realized, was frozen. He would like to say that, indeed, he knew the story, but he would give his life to be able to change it. But there was no more room for words, no more life to give. Just the frozen emptiness around him.

A flash of his own childhood came back. The skinny underdressed boy who went to bed without supper and slept with the rumble of his guts as a lullaby. The child who did not complain because he knew the futility of any expression of joy, or pain, or hunger. The sad boy that dragged a sled while his drunk mom slept. Was she asleep? Was she dead? Better not to think. Better not to turn your head, not to swerve the tense painful neck. Just pull and shut up as you always do. Don't turn around. Don't turn around. She's asleep. Asleep in the badly tanned moose hide and wolf fur. She's asleep; it can't be any other way. But the man who walks beside him is adamant. He keeps telling him things. He cannot listen because there is a humming filling his head and his body and the whole world.

Instinctively, he searched for the old Indian's portrait in his own home's kitchen. "What the hell are you proud of, you fucking old man!?" he screamed, smashing the bottle against the wall.

Jiewa took his hand between hers and cold became so overpowering that he almost lost his conscience. He pulled his hand violently and the girl stood up to an amazing height and looked at him defiantly. Her eyes were now the hot feverish eyes of the old man in the portrait. She opened her mouth to scream something at him, but she only uttered a holler and a swarm of snowflakes surrounded him. Then it dawned on him that he had not actually moved from the side of the snowmobile.

His body was paralyzed. He could not even raise his bottle. He leaned against the machine and gave in.

VIII

"Do you know, Jiewa, where the so-called *elderly wisdom* lays? In exposing your bare scars with the humbleness and peace of admitting there is no glory or shame in them that belongs to us."

The old man dragged his chair a little bit closer to his grand-daughter's bed and supported his elbows on his lap with a tired sigh. "That's why I don't understand why it is so difficult for me to reveal all these things to you. Like the way in which I met your father. Why have I never told you about it? What illusion stops me on the edge of the truth, I don't know. But the story belongs to you, so I'm going to tell you anyway.

"Kugluktuk is a small community up North, embraced by the River Coppermine on the East and by Coronation Gulf on the West, which makes it a small peninsula. The Kugluktuk settlement, they say, is more than two thousand years old. Its population are Inuit, like your grandma Lisa. They had always lived on fishing, whaling and hunting of seals and walruses until the whites set their Hudson Bay trading post in the early twenties and rained on them like doom.

"Inuits have been our natural enemies for ages, as proven by legendary blood-spilling battles for hunting territories. But what I found in Kugluktuk that winter of nineteen seventy-eight (I won't forget the date because that is the year in which my son came into my life) was a people without identity or cohesion. Only few people lived on hunting and fishing, moving around the territory like their ancestors. Most men worked at the oil wells in the Beaufort Sea with ridiculous salaries and under the harshest conditions a human being can endure. Those who remained in town were a bunch of sullen individuals weakened by the diseases and the alcohol that white men brought along. They survived crowded in poor shacks, barely making it to the end of each day. Their spirits were no longer with them.

"And what the hell was I doing in Kugluktuk? Well, that's a little bit more difficult to explain. Businesses that never thrived cause they were not meant to, because I had started them off in order to have an excuse to abandon Nogha Ti. Your grandma did not accompany me in that occasion. Sometimes she did and sometimes she didn't. By that time we had been married for several years. I met her in Yellowknife in the early seventies, way back when hippies visited us only to discover that their lifestyle was too uncomfortable above the sixtieth parallel. We both had been branded as castaways, me because of my handicap, of course, and her because she was an Inuit, which is not precisely a gurarantee of popularity among the Dogrib. She had abandoned her home in Gjoa Haven because she wanted to see the world, although the world for her, at that time, only reached to Yellowknife, where she got herself a good job sewing in a parka store. When we married, she moved into Nogha Ti and she has never complained about her decision, but then again, she was not brought up to complain.

"When years passed and children did not come, we accepted that we would never be parents. This was no drama in our relationship. We were two adults that loved each other and enjoyed each other's company, our long silent conversation, the laughter, the easy natural understanding, but family and friends accosted us with questions about when would we produce offspring. I could feel their heavy stares that seemed to say, 'look at this useless wreck of a man, unable to have children.' Perhaps it was more in my head than in theirs, but I could never get used to the humdrum of voices in our backs and the false sympathy stares. By nineteen seventy-eight, as you can imagine, I was already getting used to it, but to be honest, it was always good to take a little trip every now and then to a place where nobody knew me. My store provided me with good excuses to give wings to my spirit of adventure and fly away occasionally. Which took me to Kugluktuk in that precise moment. No sooner and no later, but right in the winter of nineteen seventy-eight.

"It was one of those glorious arctic nights, when the sky is loaded with tiny ice crystals that distort the lamp posts lights into fancy shapes. One of those nights in which you used to like to exhale a big breath that smelled of berries, to watch it freeze in the air and drop over your shoulders like a twinkling rain of silver sparks. You shushed me so that I could hear the noise of the tiny crystals falling onto your parka and you said with wide open eyes, 'Look grandpa, It's fairy dust!'

"You know I like to have some drinks with friends after work, tell jokes, listen to the laughter and the voices of other patrons in the bar, have a couple of smokes; in short, to disconnect with the seriousness of the day. And it's not that I dislike drinking at friends' homes, or mine, but the bar offers a perfect setup for playing and laughing, where almost every man can be himself. One sits at a bar and is not exposed to the friend's wife—or your own—to come with some chicken wings or any other elaborate snack and then have to become courteous and entertain a boring conversation about this and that and express profusely how yummy the chicken wings are. This does not happen at bars. At bars, one has no snack whatsoever, or a rancid cheap one. And that's perfectly okay because one can choose his conversation or alternatively choose to have none.

"So that evening I decided to visit Kugluktuk's only bar, a dark log cabin that smelled of beer sweat and smoke. Way back then, you could smoke at bars, believe it or not. This was casually called Old McNally's bar, since McNally himself was the owner and operator of the place. A mean Scottish who probably ended up in Kuguktuk after committing some despicable crime in his country, McNally (if that was his actual name), sometimes served stale peanuts on his sticky counter, but mostly we drank ale standing or sitting on stools by the bar, because the four tables were always occupied by semi-unconscious patrons that languished by their drinks, their blood-injected eyes lost in nothingness. But if one got to oversee this—which was indeed a big overseeing—one could have some laughs with friends.

"On my way out, still with the glee of the jokes and the whisky in my body, I saw a nine or ten year-old kid pulling a sled that looked very heavy. Way too heavy for his size and age. As I told you, it was a very cold night. Must have been fifty below. Even colder if you added the wind chill. It was almost eleven p.m. and, against all logic, there was that child arching his little body against the wind, trying to pull the sled. The scene shocked me. It seemed dislocated, so to say. I approached the kid, alarmed by my animal instincts that told me that something was very very wrong, and I asked, 'D'you need any help, bloke?' The kid stopped and stared at me warily.

"'No. It's my mother. She's too drunk and she fell asleep. It always happens. Every day I come to pick her up at the bar and take her home.'

"I looked into the sled more attentively. What had looked to me at first like a bunch of old blankets was actually a woman, cuddled below her caribou coat, completely blue. Frozen.

"'Wait!' I screamed, although the kid was not walking and my voice came out alarmed and sharp in spite of my efforts to look cool. I took off my right mitt and felt with a shaking hand for the woman's pulse on her neck. The flesh was cold and rigid, like a tire. It took me forever to be able to talk to the kid.

"'What's your name, son?' I asked with shaking voice, crouching beside him to look into his eyes.

"'Amorak,' said the boy, shrugging, as though he did not understand why I needed to know his name. 'It means *Wolf's Spirit*,' he clarified.

"'Amorak,' I repeated, 'Where can I find your father?' Amorak shrugged again. I nodded. 'Any other relatives, aunts, uncles, grandpa?'

"'There's only mom and me,' he said pointing at the sled with his head. Our little exchange was starting to get tense.

"'We're going to have to go to the police. Your mom is not all right.'

"Amorak, as I would later know, had been repeatedly brainwashed by his mom against the police. *They took away kids*, she had warned him. As soon as they knew their moms liked to drink, they would take them away and no one ever saw them again. They took them south, far away from their moms, to dreadful places where there were only cruel spiteful whites who did not love them. Amorak briskly stood away from me as if I had just threatened him with a knife.

"'No!' he exclaimed, throwing a sideway look at his mom. Something told him that I wasn't lying. Somehow he knew already, from his aboriginal wisdom, familiar with life and death that I was not lying. He wanted to ignore it, from his child's wisdom. "'Get away from here and leave us alone,' he said.

"But I couldn't do just that and I didn't know how to gain that child's trust. There was an abyss of incomprehension between the Dogrib and the Inuit and the abyss stank of hatred and of the spilled blood of many generations over the ice. And yet in that God forsaken place, far away from any place considered reasonable, at light-years from McDonalds and malls, a handicapped Dogrib tried desperately to tend a bridge, no matter how brittle, to the Inuit boy that was dragging his dead mom in a sled. A howling of chilly wind came up the street bringing its white shroud of snow dust. The kid and I stood there, gazing at each other clumsily, without saying anything. He didn't want to know that his mom was dead and I knew he had to, but a grief bigger than me prevented me from speaking.

"'Listen, Amorak,' I said. 'Why don't we go to the health center so that they can see your mom? See, there's no cops there. Just them nurses.' He shook his head vigorously before I finished.

"'No. Mom says that nurses are as bad as cops. They will call the cops, or the men in black from the mission. No.' Saying this, he started off again, arduously pulling his macabre cargo.

"'At least let me help you,' I said to buy some time. Since the boy didn't oppose, I threw my crutches into the sled and pushed it from behind. The wind had taken the woman's black hair from between the blankets and shook it violently like a gruesome pirate flag. In front of me, the kid advanced adamantly against the wind, checking me warily over his shoulder every few steps. Some windows poured their warm yellow light over the icy darkness of the street and I wished with all my might that someone would recognize the kid and come out to help us. There wasn't a soul in the streets or by the windows. I knew that the farther we went from the bar, the smaller my chance was to call the police or the health centre and to deliver the problem to the authorities, but I did not see how I could force that child to stop without alarming him even more. So there I was, in a land that was not mine, pushing an Inuit woman's corpse with her son, who did not know—or did not want to know—that she was dead.

"After a haul that seemed eternal, the child stopped by the door of a small rickety log cabin.

"'That's it. This is my home,' he said turning to me defiantly. 'You go now.'

"'No,' I said. 'Let me come in with you and I will help you with your mother.' He didn't answer. We placed the sled by the entrance and with a titanic effort; I half dragged the dead woman through the threshold. I still wonder how I did it. She was heavy and stiff like firewood, but I guess a man's spirit knows how to summon strength when another human being needs it. There was also my experience carrying caribou quarters with my father.

"The cabin was a single room, pervaded by the stench of a caribou carcass that rotted on the chipped linoleum floor as it was eaten in equal parts by the inhabitants of the house and the maggots. Part of the animal's meat was hanging from the beams on the ceiling, where it was getting dried to be stored. Its fat dropped directly over the floor. There was an iron stove in the corner that was used to cook and to keep the place warm. In the other corner, two beds, a closet and a camping table with two plastic chairs.

"I put the woman softly on the bed and tried to stretch her legs, but I couldn't because she was completely rigid. Her eyes were wide open and the muscle contraction had bared her teeth into a grotesque smile. I covered her face with the blanket as Amorak turned on a bare light bulb that hanged over the table and confronted me. We could not play with facts any longer.

"'Son, your mom is not passed out. She's dead,' I said simply, because I couldn't possibly come up with a softened version of the reality. As I broke the dark news, time seemed to stop. The boy dropped his arms by his sides, defeated. Then, amazingly, his resistance rose up again. He walked past me to see his mom, but fortunately he did not dare raise the blanket.

"'She's just drunk,' he said touching the rubbery covered face without removing his mittens. 'It always happens,' he repeated, trying to convince himself rather than me, but this time there was a childish shake that betrayed his voice. 'I always get her at the bar. I keep telling her to wait inside, but she goes outside the door and sits on her sled, so that I don't have to enter. Says that's no place for a child. Only today she must have sat there for a long time and she got cold. That's all. She's not dead. Mom! Mom!' he called, shaking her, and the child in me hoped against hope that she would sit up and be fine, as he was claiming. The child's voice fell apart and he stopped being the cocky little man. Skinny, helpless and scared, he started to cry.

"I ran to him and hugged him. He punched me but I did not let go. Just kept hugging him, with my eyes lost in a point way beyond the log walls, way beyond the eternal ice, way beyond the human condition, there where all the spirits are one, while I whispered sweet words in Dogrib. Slowly he surrendered to my bear hug and to his tears that ran like rivers.

"We stood there for a while, hugging each other, without needing to exchange words. The child was a child again. Loudly but trying not to alarm him, I called for help. A woman opened the door of the neighboring house. 'What is it Amorak? Your mom drunk again?' she asked mercilessly. I briefly explained the situation and the woman's husband rushed to get the police. Soon a small crowd gathered in front of the little cabin. Amorak kept clutching me like a castaway to a raft. His eyes were tightly shut and tears streamed from them, but he made no sound. Horror and grief muted him.

"Soon the heavy police Land Rover turned up, blinding us with their headlights. Two men came down unwillingly and took our statements. They entered the cabin with revulsion and stayed inside for some time until an ambulance arrived to remove the body. They exchanged some words with the paramedics and, as they were about to leave, one of them raised his arms to me in a gesture I couldn't understand at first. Then he motioned the palms of his hands upwards and I understood, horrified, that he wanted me to release the kid. I felt it was impossible to separate us in that moment. I feared the child might break in a million shards, like a delicate crystal vase. The policeman urged me, softly but firmly, to deliver the child. I tried to transfer the delicate shaking body into his arms, but he did not want to let go and the policeman ended up having to untangle his arms and legs from me, ignoring his pleads and screams. They put him in the back of the car, kicking and screaming for his mom. And as the car started, I thought with bitterness, so did Amorak's new uncertain future, in the hands of merciless southerners, as his mother had foretold.

"I walked away as fast as I could, with my heart gripped by grief. I hurried up the street wishing that Old MacNally's bar was still open. It was. The Scottish never closed until he saw the very last chance of a penny leave through his door. Two of my pals were at the bar. I came to them hungry of human warmth and I ordered a double whisky.

"'Fuck, Jimmy, what's wrong? You look like you've just seen a ghost,' said one of them.

"'Worse,' I said and sipped my drink trying to warm up my stomach and my thoughts. My friend discarded me with a move of his hand and returned to the discussion he was entertaining with the other one, about a helix engine that one wanted to sell to the other one. Their inebriated state would have been concerning since one of them was piloting the flight to take us home the next day, but I could just think of the images of the last hour, flying around me like black moths that a second drink could not scare away.

"I left a couple of bills on the bar, said goodnight and made my way to the police station.

"Amorak was being held in the *drunk tank*, the cell where they kept violent drunkards for the night. Now he seemed calmer, in a state that was almost catatonic. He was hugging his own knees and rocking back and forth, back and forth. His eyes were red and swollen. It seemed he had kicked and punched the officers profusely before being locked up, which raised my admiration for the kid. Beside him, lying in a bunk bed, an old man howled like a wolf, lost in the vapors of alcohol. Maybe he was lamenting his own pitiful state; maybe he was grieving with the kid. None of the officers were looking at Amorak. They were engrossed in a banal chat. As for the men in the drunk tank, each was locked in his own hermetic loneliness and I could not see them becoming aggressive to the kid. Probably they would be asleep or comatose in less than an hour.

"'Amorak,' I called softly from the counter, but just as I expected, he did not even acknowledge my voice. 'Is it really necessary to keep the kid locked in that cell with all those men?' The policeman looked at me briefly.

"'It is the only place where we can put him for the night, seein' as the mission is closed for some weeks,' he answered with an unfriendly stare underlined by deep purple circles. 'Do you want to join him?' he asked menacingly. I should have expected such an answer. Back then, an Indian was not supposed to have the audacity to question the authority of the police, so I didn't answer. I'd rather not draw attention to myself.

"I looked again at Amorak. His tanned face rocking in the hard light of the cell, his intense black eyes devoid of hope or emotion. 'Doesn't he have a family, friends, someone with whom he could spend the night?' I insisted.

"'Don't you think he has enough friends?' asked the other cop with a smile, pointing at the other inmates with a broad gesture of his hand, and they both laughed. I understood that the child was alone, that his alcoholic now deceased mom had probably not made lots of friends and that nobody was going to help him.

"'Listen, I have a room,' I said timidly. 'I can take him with me. He will be better there, don't you think?'

"'Fucking pervert,' muttered one of them, the comedian one, turning around to shuffle some papers, while the other answered, annoyed. 'See, right now there is nothing we can do. Tomorrow morning the Justice of Peace will be here to assess the situation. Then you can talk to him and he will make the decision. Until then, the kid will not move from here. Now I'm gonna ask you to leave this office or I shall have to lock you with the gang there,' he said pointing at the cell with his head.

"I promptly followed his advice, but as I was exiting the police station I had already made up my mind to adopt Amorak, your father. Because should I not do it, I knew his ghost and his mother's would follow me till old age and I have never been prone to cultivate nightmares.

"Funny enough, the process was easier than I had expected. The next day I was at the police station, freshly shaved, waiting for the Justice of Peace. He showed up around ten-thirty. He was a chunky man in his early sixties. He was wearing a beaver hat and a fur coat that made him look like a strange caveman. He sat for a while to fill up forms with the policemen. Finally one of them pointed at me with his chin and the man stood up nodding and came to me with heavy strides, as he pretended to be reading some forms.

"I realized at once that, luckily for me, this was a tired man, prone to solving problems as fast as possible. He slumped with a wheeze on the wooden bench beside me and looked at me with watery eyes. He panted all the time, as though the mere effort of living were too much for him and his face was congested, full of broken capillaries, especially on his bulbous nose.

"He studied me silently and then he spoke. 'Are you a relative of the minor?' he asked without introducing himself. I shook my head and I proceeded to tell him all the events of the previous night which he listened with a profusion of head shaking and tsking of his tongue in disapproval.

"'Looks like the child has no relatives or anyone who would take care of him,' I explained. 'I don't have any children.' I said almost apologetically, 'so I would happily adopt Amorak.'

"'Just like that?' the judge asked briskly, arching his eyebrows in amazement. I shrugged and did not answer the incongruous question.

"'I am going to be totally honest to you,' he finally said, his face close enough to mine for me to smell the stale whisky in his breath. 'You will understand that under normal circumstances, we should never agree to your request. There is a series of legal procedures required for an adoption, which are normally managed by the missionaries at Saint Andrew. But as it happens, they are not in Kugluktuk, but spreading the... Lord's word in other communities, and we do not expect them back until early spring. Until then, we do not have a suitable place to place the child, so you happen to have showed up in the very right moment.' He forced a festive expression that did not match the situation at all. Then he remained pensive for a moment, turning his beaver hat in his hands on his lap.

"'On the other hand,' he continued, 'since I am not authorized to process the adoption, you may take the minor under the understanding that the ministers might claim him should a relative come up asking for him, which I doubt, or should they want to place him in an orphanage. The officers will take your name and address and you can take the child with you.' I agreed, smiling. I was pretty sure nobody would claim that poor devil, and it never happened. The issue was settled.

"'Now,' he added with a severe expression, without looking at me in the eye. 'There are certain processing expenses you would have to...'

"'How much?' I asked, feeling sorry for the man and eager to get out of that place.

"'Forty dollars,' he said longingly.

"'I only have thirty,' I lied, taking the bills out of my pocket. The man picked them up briskly and put them in his coat's pocket while looking at the agents sideways. He stood up and offered me a swollen limp hand that I shook dutifully.

"'Well, very pleased to meet you, Mr…'

"'Whitefox, Jimmy Whitefox,' I said.

"The Judge went to the counter to give some directions to the police officers. Then he turned around and nodded at me with a smile that said *Nice to do business with you, Mr. Whatever* and he left. As I saw him get out to the cold morning wrapped in furs he had not hunted, I wondered at how could they call that man Justice of Peace. A man who had delivered a child and his destiny into my hands without even knowing my name. But you will see, Jiewa, that among the white men there are totally useless, or even harmful human beings, that occupy high responsibility positions in their society without being replaced and given a more adequate task to their capacity or nature.

"Anyway, the thing is one of the policemen called me with an impatient shake of his hand and made me sit in front of him to gather my personal information. As I answered his questions, I was certain he would throw the paper in his dustbin as soon as we were done. *That's even better*, I thought. Way back then, one did not want to be in the police files for any reason whatsoever.

"Once we were done with the paperwork farce, he took his keys from a hook on the wall, opened the cell and took Amorak out. He was dirty and exhausted, but he was now conscious of his environment.

"'Do you know who I am?' I asked him, leaning to look him in the eye, and he nodded. I held his arm softly and escorted him out of that somber place. We walked in silence to the restaurant, where I ordered a breakfast worth of a king for him, with eggs, pancakes with syrup, bacon and sausages… the whole works. The child devoured the food without raising his eyes from the plate. When he was done, his face looked much better and he assessed me with curiosity instead of distrust.

"Since he didn't ask any questions, I told him, 'Amorak, you are coming to Nogha Ti with me. You don't need to go South with the whites.' He nodded nonchalantly, as though we were not talking about his future but somebody else's. 'Well, it'll be a little bit South, but not *that* south,' I added to honour the truth. 'And as you can see, I ain't no white man.' This unnecessary affirmation made him smile.

"He did not ask anymore about his mother. Ever. I asked if he wanted to have a bath to remove the stench of the cell and he gave me a wary look, so I let it be. His new mom would be in charge of that when we arrived in Nogha Ti. That very afternoon we flew to Yellowknife. I observed, amused, his euphoria, his big amazed eyes as he saw and felt himself airborne, his face stuck to the window. I saw myself so many years ago in my first flight with Father Tyrone and I smiled at the wonder of our encounter. I was rescuing Amorak in the exact same way as I had been rescued so many years ago. These things are never coincidence, Jiewa. These things close circles that often we do not understand. Circles that seem ours, but in most cases leave us outside, wondering with stupid faces."

IX

Four turquoise wounds cross the jet black sky as if a giant invisible bear had clawed the shielding curtain of the night revealing a ghostly extraterrestrial glow on the other side. Then the lines snake smoothly in different directions, alternating colours and shapes. Sometimes they seem blown by the wind, sometimes they seem alive, massive radiant anacondas banishing darkness and death; astral beasts dragging myriads of purple and topaz fire scales, spilling their impossible, almost liquid light over the vast arctic desolation: The Northern Lights, or Nah-Kaah, as the Dogrib call it. One can watch them in silence and listen to their hiss, feel their sulphur smell. And witnessing their unbelievable beauty, you can wonder how can a man die of exposure under the sign of such a unique prodigy. How sad will be the admiring smile of the dying man who contemplates the sky open like a flower on his last bed over the infinite snow.

The blizzard is now over. It has withdrawn, its thirst of fear and death quenched, and Jimmy listens to the crunching of the steps over the virgin dawn snow before he hears the door open. Smooth steps, steps for a day of pain, steps of solidarity and comfort. The first neighbors have arrived. The death parade has begun and he should be joining it, but somehow he doesn't believe his legs will hold him if he stands up. Not sure that he can face this day, close the anguish in his chest, raise his head and speak in a firm voice to thank for the support.

"Not yet," he moans.

But the voices of the newly arrived make themselves heard downstairs. The kitchen noises, the dragging of chairs, the smell of bannock. Everything is so slow.

Jiewa squirms smoothly under the sheets. She can unconsciously listen to all these noises. Jimmy leans over her and blows softly on her ear, but she turns around and keeps sleeping. Always the sleepyhead this one, Jimmy chuckles. Well, no reason to wake her up. What's the hurry? Death has all the time in the world.

He, on the other hand, might not have so much time, so he hurries to continue telling his story.

"'Somebody has killed all my dogs,' screamed the old man with a harsh voice and eyes reddened by crying. The cold white light of the office made his deeply wrinkled face a text that told his story as a hunter and a trapper in the Arctic. The deep creases that seemed cut by a knife, the leathery texture of his caramel coloured neck and hands, washed enough to move in a white men's world, the strong bone structure of his face, crisp and defined, almost that of a young man. The face of a man who cannot abandon himself to the smoothness of old age because he knew that there is no abandonment without death.

"Over his strong crooked nose, some metal framed glasses would tell you, though, that this old Dogrib had been happily integrated in the 'civilized' system and would not have to go to die in the hole in the snow, as his parents and their parents did when they stopped being able to fend for themselves. This old Dogrib had a pension, a log cabin with electricity and water, medical insurance, an apology from the Canadian Government for previous genocides.

"Tom, the Senior Administrative Officer, had not heard him enter. Startled, he spun around in his chair to meet the stormy glare of the old man. Non-natives are normally exasperated at the Dogribs' inborn ability to move like hunters. They do not hear us or see us until they have us right in front of them. It doesn't matter if we're wearing heavy snow boots or sneakers. Our walking integrates with the whole, it blends with the environment. It is as simple as knowing the nature of the soil you step on, the acoustic of every space, the direction of the wind. To be conscious of your environment, of the situation in which you are moving every precise moment. Not to be wandering around in daydream. That's why a white man cannot see a Dogrib in the street, or the forest, or wherever, without the Dogrib having seen him first. If it looks like he has not seen him, it is probably the wrong perception: he has seen him, but has nothing in particular to tell him, so he continues on. This ghostly quality of the Dogribs makes white men very nervous, for they walk immersed in thoughts that are not from the present, with their gaze lost far away from reality, so that when you bring it back to them, it will often startle them. Or worse, sometimes it is a hungry bear that catches them unawares.

"On that particular day, Tom wondered, irritated, why his secretary had not announced the presence of the elder. But, of course, he was an elder and elders' actions are not questioned or announced by anyone in Dogrib society. Tom had been immersed in the tedious preparation of an endless budget which ramifications seemed to know no end when he was so brusquely interrupted. He was speechless at first, trying to process the striking question, trying to find an immediate response, frequent obsession among 'civilized' men. Dogs? For a long moment, the abstract realm of figures had taken him from the peculiar reality of that place.

"Of course. Dogs. The answer came like a gust of wind or a slap. The previous week, by decision of the Council, the RCMP had been entrusted with the nasty task of killing all the abandoned dogs in town. This was done every year because otherwise the hungry beasts gathered in packs like wolves to search for food, attack children, and spread garbage all over town.

"Sometimes the wolves themselves kill the wild dogs. They venture into town at night when the winter is really hard and the hunting is difficult and eat all the animals that are outside. There is nothing that could be compared to their howling in the immense loneliness of the arctic night. Profound, cold, obscure blood-curdling howlings that invoke the most arcane fears in human spirits. One, two, three, then many wolf voices howling hungrily just by your house. By your children. You can even see the red spots of their eyes through your window and you know that everyone in town is feeling just like you. Only a few dogs survive these raids. The rest are eaten and only the heads are left behind. By the way, Jiewa, your dog is going to follow that destiny very soon, always tied far away from the house, poor animal.

"But in the year I'm talking about, a rather big group of dogs had survived hunger, winter and wolves and were roaming around, scaring the children, eating the fish or caribou meat that women lay outside to dry, and spreading garbage all over town.

"The nasty task of killing them had been entrusted to the new RCMP officer, Peter Whaler, a young boy from Newfoundland, about twenty-two, but looked seventeen. He wore his uniform with proud neatness, crowning it with a military crew cut of his velveteen golden hair. His face was childish and his blue gaze placid and transparent. In spite of his too obvious efforts to convey toughness and courage, when looking at him one could imagine him folding with care his socks and underwear, or ironing his shirts with zeal, or eating his Quaker Oats sitting at an impeccable little table in his kitchen, already dressed for duty. Never would you see him pointing a gun at someone or kicking a drunk into the drunk tank.

"When his sergeant gave him the task of terminating the stray dogs, he deeply disliked it. He was an RCMP Officer, not a dog killer. But of course, he got the 'job' for being the newest and youngest in the detachment, and he had to obey orders. So that morning, probably after eating his Quaker Oats and brushing his teeth, he had taken his riffle, mounted the patrol car, slammed the door a tad too hard and started the shameful hunting.

"He killed eight stray dogs, and it was not easy, I tell you. First of all, he had to lasso them, and those elusive motherfuckers seemed to know his intentions. They were shrewd and wolfish, and hunger made their instincts more aware of danger. Once he captured them, he had to take them to the dump and shoot them, feeling miserable every time. Sometimes, when he could not capture them, he had to shoot them on site, and that was the worst. The desperate agony screams that sounded almost human, the wide open eyes full of panic and pain.

"To make it worse, people gave him ugly looks as he did his job. They did not want those hungry beasts prowling around their children, but they neither liked to see the village cop shooting at them. It was a woeful show, that's for sure, especially because of the Dogrib People's respect for dogs. For generations they have helped us to survive on the ice, to haul camp following the migrations of the game, to protect the meat stashes from wolves and bears. This kind of relationship is not easily forgotten, for it goes in our blood. I wonder, Jiewa, if you still have this memory in your soul, of how your dogs' peaceful presence outside the tent banished beasts and nightmares, of how just a gentle affectionate poke of your dog's wet nose can make you perceive the world as a much friendlier place."

Jimmy looks at Jiewa's forehead intently, wishing that, by doing so, he could read her thoughts and feelings, spy the dreams that dance around her sleeping head. How had she become such a stranger when he loves her so much?

"Besides," he continues, "us Dogribs believe that if you kill a dog, its spirit will come back to stalk you children, so it's the police who have to shoot these abandoned animals. The locals would consider it very bad luck to do it themselves. And there was poor Peter Whaler, crimson red, huffing and puffing in pursuit of all those dogs, and probably wishing that one of the irate onlookers would draw the nerve of shouting something at him, so that he could answer back expressing his frustration in a fair way. But a cop is not authorized to punish a dirty look." Jimmy could not avoid giggling at the thought.

"Poor Peter finished the job and was back at the police office at about three in the afternoon. The sergeant noticed his somber expression while he furiously tried to rub a persistent stain of blood off his otherwise impeccable jacket. He patted young Whaler's shoulder, laughing and gave him permission to take the rest of the day off. Peter thanked him and said he would rather go on a patrol over the lake. The quietness and silence would wipe the ugly death memories from his head

"Patrolling the lake was—and still is—a really futile exercise of RCMP in an attempt to prevent alcohol and marijuana bootlegging aboard the boats, which is actually an impossible mission, even though they know exactly who the bootleggers and weed dealers are and what boats they own. Not once have they gotten any of them red-handed. See, those guys know the lake, which is the size of a European country, like the back of their hand. They are as skillful as any fish when it comes to navigating the islet mazes and if, in spite of that, the RCMP ever got sight of one of them, they just have to throw the 'goods' overboard and wave smilingly at them. And yet the police still do the lake patrol. Why they do is a mystery to me.

"But the fact is that particular afternoon, this practice seemed very appealing to Corporal Whaler. A perfect way to escape the shitty day and enjoy the peace of the lake. He jumped into the boat and started the engine. It sounded familiar and trustworthy, hardly bothering the crystalline silence of the lake. He sat at the comfortable padded seat and, as he held the steering wheel, his shoulders relaxed automatically, letting go of the rest of the world as the boat opened its way slowly, leaving a gurgling trail over the perfectly transparent water.

"In his first lake patrols, he had not felt very secure. The lake was huge and splashed with hundreds of tiny islets that made it very easy to get lost. With time, he was learning to differentiate them by their position, the amount of trees in them and their shape, and now he could actually use them for orientation and to locate those dangerous parts where the water was shallower. That day, he decided to take his time and inspect a pass, hardly seven yards wide, that went through a very long peninsula and was used by the fishermen to access what they said was one of the best fishing spots in the lake. He located the pass, turned off and hoisted the engine onboard, for the pass was hardly two feet deep. He used the oar to push his way through the rocks and, once on the other side, he took some minutes to orientate himself and take some reference points for his return. That was when he heard them.

"At first he thought it was a figment of his imagination, a product of the exhaustion and distress of the day, like when one closes the eyes in front of a powerful source of light and can still see the shapes against the back of one's eyelids. In a conscious effort, he tried to make the sound fade in his own mind, to make it not exist, in a way. However, in spite of his efforts to rationalize his senses, the barking continued. Peter tried to convince himself they were not real, but they persisted. After some minutes, he was sure they were very real and they came from an islet on his right, at approximately seven hundred yards. He steered his boat in that direction and when he was close enough, he could see, in amazement, some more of those wolfish faces that were branded in his brain after his, never better said, dog's day. He was stupefied. The islet could not be more than twenty yards wide. There could not be two dogs there. Then, a third one appeared, leaning his forepaws on a rock. How the hell had they reached there? Was he hallucinating? 'What the fuck!' he whispered, breaking his vow not to ever swear. The dog leaning on the rock seemed to call him with two short shrill barks, followed by an eerie howl. A shiver shook Peter's body. He slowed down, for the water was very shallow around there and the bottom of the lake was covered in sharp rocks.

"He was now fifteen yards from the islet and could count five dogs in that outlandish place. Hungry, skinny, sick, with lacerated dirty fur. Now they were looking at him anxiously. If he stopped and left the boat they would jump on him and devour him. Or perhaps not. Perhaps they needed affection even more than food. But no. Judging by their state, the devouring option seemed much more likely.

"The five wolfish faces stayed fixed on him, in still expectation, even as they ran up and down on the shore rocks, nervously calculating his intent, his weight, perhaps his taste. Whaler contemplated them back in awe. He studied them and they studied him, calculating the impossible way of covering the distance that separated them from the man. The sound of their panting and groaning was almost tangible in the silence of the lake.

"Now, maybe if he had come across this unfortunate pack on a different day, Whaler would have shaken his head and turned around, but not on this day, he couldn't. He shot all of them, one by one. It was not difficult because there was no hiding place in the islet. The shots sounded like cannon blasts, suffocating the dying howling, and he kept shooting and shooting until he ran out of ammunition. The silence that followed as the vibrations receded on the fresh indifferent air, was a silence of peace. The lake was now more perfect without the useless suffering of those five animals weighing like lead over its tranquil beauty.

"A couple of days later, the sergeant asked him to go to the Hamlet Office, since the Administrator needed to see him. Whaler drove there unwillingly. When they called you from Hamlet Office it was normally about some stupid quarrel about a drunk bothering a secretary in the Band office, or someone who had stolen petty cash, or someone who had thrown an egg on someone's window, where it would remain frozen until the spring, which was the favorite local prank. He parked his Land Rover by the office and entered the building. As he came into Tom's office and saw the devastated old man and the Administrator's distressed expression, he knew that no petty cash was going to be discussed that day. I was also already there. The secretary had phoned me to come and help my father.

"'Thank you for coming, Peter,' the Administrator said, almost in a sigh, obviously alleviated by his presence. 'Mr. Joe Whitefox here was explaining to me that today he went to the islet where he used to keep his sled dogs for the spring and summer and he found them all shot dead. It came to my mind that you were shooting stray dogs the other day and I was wondering if you might have... you know?'

"Peter was speechless. So the dogs did belong to someone who had not actually abandoned them. How come he had never considered this? The animals had obviously not made it to the islet on their own and it was pretty unlikely for someone to take the bother of getting there to abandon five dogs. The anguish of the day had clouded his thinking. He was in trouble. He turned his hat in his hand for a long moment, unable to give an answer, trying unsuccessfully to keep his cheeks from blushing. He looked like a kid in front of the Principal.

"'I'm so sorry. I really thought they were abandoned. They were starved, sick. I just wanted to take them out of their misery.' he finally managed to say. 'I just could not think they belonged to someone. Just could never occur to me. I'm so sorry. I was told to shoot on all the abandoned dogs because they are dangerous for the kids, and these were the most abandoned of all. So I...'

"'But these dogs were not a danger to anyone!' roared my father, kicking childishly on the floor. His voice came out shrill and full of anguish. He swore in Dogrib. 'My dogs were in the islet. They harmed no one there! They were my dogs! Who will pull my sled this winter? How am I going to get me some firewood? How am I going to tend to my snares?'

"'But you can't leave them abandoned in those conditions,' replied Whaler with all the tenderness he was capable of. 'It's inhumane. They were suffering...'

"'Suffering!' my father scoffed bitterly. 'What do you know about suffering? You've spent your life in the whites' schools and in police stations with heating, sipping coffee and eating packed cookies. What the hell do you know about chasing the caribou on the ice, of seeing your relatives die of exposure or hunger? The dogs were suffering...' he mimicked mockingly. 'I also suffer,' he said with a defeated voice. 'But I needed those dogs and they needed me. I took them to the islet because I don't have much to feed them and here they would look for food. Make trouble. They would open the garbage cans, or attack the children. But I took them fish to the islet. Fish that I could have eaten.' He looked at each of them with an unbearable sadness in his eyes. 'I also suffer,' he repeated. 'They didn't suffer more than me.' He wiped off his face with the back of his hand, raised his hood, stood up and went out without goodbye, leaving a strong smell of smoked fish and chicory in the room. Whaler and Tom looked at each other with dismay.

"The three of us remained in silence. Poor Peter seemed about to start to cry, so Tom spoke in an energetic tone. 'Don't worry, Peter, you just did what you were told.' He noticed the stupidity of the sentence just as he was saying it. Peter nodded with the same lack of conviction.

"'Don't worry, guys. I will take him his firewood this winter,' I said, standing up to leave.

"'No.' Peter cut in, staring at me with reddened eyes. 'I will,' and murmuring a goodbye, he left the office in a hurry lest we could see the tears welling up.

"I found my father sitting on the wooden bench on the office porch, his stare lost on the lake beyond the plain. He had a Styrofoam cup with hot tea in his hands, more to keep them warm than to drink the liquid. I sat down beside him and, for the first time in my life, I saw his gnarled hands shake. The hunter of so many arctic winters, the great man whose respect I had pursued in vain in my childhood and youth was now sunken. The man I had seen with my own eyes fight even when he was in the jaws of a Kodiak bear was now shaking, scared, lost in a world that was not his anymore, a world he could not manage.

"I remember I thought, will he now understand me, now that circumstances have matched us as two beings that, through the natural course of life, would not have the right to be living? Will he understand now the grief of losing one's roots? After a lifetime of estrangement, my father and I had finally something in common, and it was the pain of loss, but not even this could we share, for I would never have gathered the cruelty to present these thoughts to him and neither would he have deigned discussing them.

"I ached to grab his shaking hand and warm it up in mine, to comfort the once powerful crooked fingers of the hunter. But I knew better than to try to hold his hand. Even in weakness there was a cautious distance between us, a cordial distance that would never be crossed. Things between us were like that. Just so. That's why that day on that bench facing the lake, not grabbing his shaking hand was a show of respect, not indifference.

"He drank his tea in silence, regaining his grip and his calm. Then he stood up, crushed the cup, dropped it in the garbage can and we made our way to his home, the noises of the little streams of water from the thaw surrounding us, the whiskey jays darting all over the place in the fragrant air of a spring that did not belong to the old hunter anymore, that had never belonged to me.

"'I'm coming with you to tend to the nets,' I said.

"'No,' he said shaking his head vigorously. 'I already did this morning. That's how I found out...' he couldn't finish the sentence, and I nodded.

"'Father,' I said after a long silence, 'this winter you can use my ski-doo with the toboggan to bring the wood and tend to the traps. It is very easy to drive. It will be fun.'

"But his expression indicated he could not see the fun in it. We both knew he was too old to train another dog team, that he would never have another dog team and that was another chapter of his life that was stolen by the white men and the storm of unrequested changes they brought along. Now he would have to suffer the humiliation of letting his own son teach him to fend for himself in a world of white men, with the white men's machines one had to pay with slavery to the banks."

Jimmy leans over his granddaughter to look at her up close, listen to her breath, feel her spirit for there might be no more occasions.

"I hope you understand, Jiewa," he continues, "that although this encounter with my father was in despair and disorientation, it was the most intimate encounter we ever shared. Unbelievable, eh? But that was the closest I have ever been to the Hunter. My father was a very proud man. He had to fall in order for us to meet face to face. It sounds terrible, but sometimes it is like that. And I don't know if it's necessarily bad when it's like that. I don't know if what we call losing is always necessarily losing."

X

Jimmy recognizes the heavy vaguely martial steps. The snow hardly muffles the noise of the boots on the landing wooden floor. He walks to the window, but he does not need to look to check that two RCMP officers are standing in front of the door. Their hats are in their hands. He shuts his eyes tightly, so tightly they hurt, and he grinds his teeth, as a man getting ready to have a wound cauterized with a red hot knife.

Everything is so shrill, so pungently sharp. The policemen knock on the door and the murmur in the living room is interrupted by a dense silence. He hears his daughter-in-law's steps to the door, which she opens. He listens to the officers' voices without wanting to listen, without wanting any word to bite his flesh and remain there forever like an ice shard. His fists are so tight that his fingernails are hurting his palms and his arms shake. He finally feels weak. He finally feels like an old man. The hex is done and there is no escaping the void that follows.

When he gets to relax the tension in his neck, he turns his face to his granddaughter and calls with a neutral strong voice that does not seem his, that is not his.

"Jiewa, wake up."

She frowns, turns her head a couple of times and opens two small sleepy slits.

"Grampa?" she says hoarsely.

"Time to wake up," he says trying to keep his voice from shaking.

"What the hell are you doing here? There's no school today. Let me sleep," she groans as she covers herself up to the nose in the blankets.

This is his Jiewa, his stubborn warrior.

"It's your father," he says, his voice sinking. "He took off from Yellowknife yesterday evening and was caught in the blizzard." He could tell the whole news, open the horror box. But his strength fails him. After all, he thinks with some resentment, his mom beyond tears is downstairs. She can update her. But the girl understands and sits up abruptly, checking that the Eminem T-shirt properly covers her generous curves.

"You been here for a while, eh," she says

"A good while, yeah," he answers. "Couldn't find a better place to wait."

"Get out so I can get dressed," she says, looking at him warily. He nods and, fighting stiffness takes his crutches and gets out of the room, closing the door behind him. Outside, in the landing, his grandson Edzo is looking at him dazed. He is wearing some jeans and has a t-shirt in his hand.

"The cops came here? Whassup?" he asks. Jimmy quiets him with a gesture.

"C'mon. Help me down these friggin' stairs, will you?" he asks with infinite weariness.

As they go down, he becomes the focus of the stares of the many people who are already gathered in the living room. Like the star in a musical show. Perhaps they need to see someone who does cry, to witness some grief. His heart tries to linger on the warm dimness of his granddaughter's bedroom, on his own memories, on anything that brings warmth to his soul. But there is no returning to warmth or to memories.

His daughter-in-law approaches him with her tearless furious eyes and she says, "He's dead." She stands there for a moment, awaiting the old man to answer or drop dead, but none of this happens and she comes back to the comfort of the crowd gathered in her kitchen. Jimmy holds on to his grandson's arm. Only Edzo knows how tight. He doesn't want to let go because he is sure that his weak disabled legs will let go and he will fall down. Edzo feels this fear because he holds him tighter and Jimmy gives himself to his care, to the compassion of his grandson.

People keep respectfully silent while grandfather and grandson cross the living room to the sofa. Then a luminous presence approaches him discreetly: Lisa, his wife. Small, rounded, wet in tears, she cuddles beside him, warming up his heart without the need of words, as she has always done. Jimmy is taken aback by the power of her reassuring presence. Her slanted Inuit eyes that are smiling by nature are now dense, grave, and opaque.

Lisa had not stolen his heart, as the white woman once did. She simply had sat on a quiet corner of his home without asking for permission, to sew jackets, boots, mukluks and mitts, as she had always done. And her presence had grown and grown around him like a giant aura that enveloped everything in warmth. Slowly, all objects, colors and lights took her personality and the home became her. Coming back home was coming back to her laughter, her chicory smell, the small noise of her scissors and the hissing of the furs she was working on. Now Jimmy could not conceive a home without her, a home that was not her, but if someone asked why, he would not be able to tell.

In the suffocating living room, but somehow far away from the crowd that gathers around them, husband and wife brace together, with their hands tightly clasped, waiting for the moment to pass. The first moment, the most dangerous one. That moment when small details, sharp and insignificant, like a sentence, or a face, or a smell, can worm into one's heart like larvae and stay there forever, like massive holes in the ice that can swallow a whole man.

XI

Death, as much as life, is a great event for the Dogrib. When someone dies, dozens of people from other communities pour in to attend funerals and burials. Accommodation must be arranged and meals must be set up for all the guests. Even though everyone helps, it involves a great deal of hard work. The encounter always ends up becoming festive. A celebration of life for those who are still alive.

The missionaries had proclaimed ever since they laid foot in Nogha Ti, that it was imperative to bury the dead; what's more, even if they died hunting far away in the bush, they had to be buried all together in the same place which is called a cemetery and is considered holy ground, as if the rest of the ground was not holy, too. Then the permafrost problem arose up. A layer of frozen ground, harder than concrete, that lays beneath the ice for most of the year, making it impossible to dig a grave.

For many years, those who had the discourtesy of dying during the winter were stored without ceremony in a casket in the cemetery's toolshed, where they remained frozen until the thaw allowed any digging.

These days, thanks to the sophisticated bulldozers, this unsettling corpse storage was no longer used. Although Jimmy thought it was somehow irreverent, even sacrilegious, to have the massive yellow machines pushing, stirring, and stomping on the so-called holy ground.

Six men carried his son's casket towards the cemetery, followed by the parade that advanced silently. Only the crunching of the snow and the cawing of the ravens could be heard as they approached the church. His granddaughter Jiewa advanced silently by her brother. She had not spoken since she received the news and although he had not seen her cry, he noticed her eyes were reddened and this appeased him because he knew tears were made to wash, and wherever they run it is never in vain.

The funeral was fast because a frozen wind was beginning to rise again. The family, led as a team by Jimmy's sister Adelle, had prepared a feast with caribou stew and bannock in the social centre, a big square building made of wood and glass that was used for gatherings. Soon all the guests were there, with the steaming bowls in their hands. Jimmy felt relieved that this was the last social ritual related to his son's death. Finally he could retreat to his home to lick his wounds. Finally there would be silence and he could snuggle in the protective presence of his wife, the furniture, the lamps, and the known crockery. No more hugs, no more handshakes, no more condolences, please. After all this organized chaos, his son would become at last his personal intimate memory he could weep about whenever he pleased.

In order to follow the protocol, he took a stew bowl. The heat and the smell were comforting. He picked up a bannock and went unwillingly to sit by Cynthia, his daughter-in-law, not because this idea appealed him at all, but because he did not want to reject the woman in public. Rejection of a woman by a respected elder was a very fast spreading condition and he meant no harm to her. As soon as he sat down, he could feel her tense up. Revulsion is never unilateral. Her breath smelled strongly of alcohol and as soon as he perceived it, he knew it had been a mistake to sit down beside her.

"Hah! What an undeserved honor!" she said bitterly, drawing disapproval glares from the other diners, even from her own relatives. One is not supposed to speak disrespectfully at a Dogrib elder, especially if that one is a woman. Jimmy nodded and started to eat his stew. The woman's tension was spreading around her like a forest fire, pulling the air and the silence. Where was Lisa, anyway? She had a special knack for relieving tense situations. Why was his wife not beside him, talking about this and that with the rest of the guests? The old man dutifully finished his lunch, murmured goodbyes to the people at the table and tried to keep his composure for the rest of the gathering, counting the long minutes until he could politely retire to his home to meet his pain alone.

That night, as Lisa was helping him to put on his pajamas, he told her about his encounter with Cynthia and he reproached her. "Where the hell were you? How could you leave me alone at the table with that witch?"

Lisa stopped for a moment and looked at him apologetically.

"I wanted to go, but my legs didn't," she explained. Then Jimmy realized he had spent the last days seeking her support, without considering that this was her loss, too. He was so used to leaning on her, to counting on her balance and serenity, that it had become a natural fact.

"I'm sorry," he said.

She did not answer. He thought about asking her how did she feel, but he already knew: fucked. He hugged her. There was nothing so soft and so welcoming in the world as her embrace.

"She will come back to you," Lisa said, as she fluffed her pillows and took her sewing from the nightstand. "She will come back because she is going to need your help now that she's widowed. Give her some days for the rage to cool down and go see her." Jimmy stared at her while she beaded a beautiful flower pattern on a mitten, hooking every bead with a tiny needle. Normality was her way of coping, he thought. Routine was her sedative and ultimately his own sedative, too. The rhythmic moves of the muscles in her chubby arms as she sewed appeased him like a nightmare-proof lullaby.

"Lisa," he said

"Hmm?" she asked

"Do you know how important you are for me?"

She stopped for a moment and turned her rounded face to him with an almost smile. Not her habitual overflown Inuit smile, but a smile after all.

"Yes," she simply said, and kept working. Jimmy nodded. After all, not everything was over and not all women looked at him like an old man.

XII

"So, when are you going to visit them?" Lisa asked without raising her eyes from the mukluks she was sawing.

"Whom?" he asked irritated, pretending to be engrossed in the hunting and fishing program on TV. Lisa kept sewing without answering. The only light in the room, apart from the intermittent gloom from the TV was the lamp in her sewing corner, which gave her the appearance of an illuminated chubby oracle, like a small Northern Buddha.

"Nobody in that house is happy to see me," he said moodily. "What's the point in me going?" The truth was, two weeks had passed since the funeral and no contact had been made between them.

"They need money, Jimmy, and you know they aren't going to ask you."

"It's easy for you to talk. Nobody gets angry at you because… because it's impossible," he said, frustrated, "but that family is furious with me."

"It's not *that family*, but *your family* and they have reasons to be angry at both of us. We should have done something while we still had time," she said with her gaze lost far away, in the land of the dead, where the password for the living is always *should have*.

"Like what!" shouted Jimmy, slapping his thigh. "I gave them money. Lots of money, and they were eager to drink it away. Cynthia too, by the way," he pointed out wagging an accusing index finger. "I kept nagging Amorak and her but there was nothing to be done. As soon as he set a foot out of the mine he was drunk or drugged or whatever he was into, until his holiday shift was over. I even offered him to go to Edmonton to a rehab clinic that I would have paid and, by the way, was not cheap, and he told me he could not do that because he could not leave his family. Hah! What a joke. And what about her? I offered to bring the kids to live with us so they could be safe, but that was not fine either. They just wanted money. I kept passing it and they kept drinking it."

"But when Jiewa asked you to…"

"Ask what?" he screamed really hurt. "When she asked me to put my own son in jail? What kind of father would do that?"

"He'd be better in jail than dead," Lisa said, regretting her own words as she was uttering them. Jimmy picked up his crutches and left the room without a word. A part of Lisa urged her to follow him and apologize, give him a hug, prepare supper, give him back the normality he was longing for. But another part of her, one much more resentful and unexplored, kept her there, in her illuminated corner, with her hands crossed on her lap and her gaze lost in the blackness of the window, remembering that she had wanted to speak in court that time and Jimmy had forbidden her to do so and now nothing would bring her son back. Nor the respect of her daughter-in-law and grandchildren.

She remembered with a rancor almost unknown to her, the elders of the Nogha Ti gathering at her dining room table with solemn arrogance, palavering about the destiny of his son and grandchildren with Jimmy, not with her. She had not been allowed to take part in that macabre cabal, for not only she was a woman, but also she was Inuit, the enemy's offspring, so her silence and submission were taken for granted since the elders entered into her house. Her house. Her son.

"The police," Robert Nitsawa had said, "are not like us. They are not our brothers. They belong in the white men's world. Your granddaughter is defying the community in her desire to go to them for help. Why did she not come to us first? Has she forgotten where she belongs and who are her elders? We are capable of solving the issues in our community. It has always been like that." They all considered carefully his words for some minutes.

"Since when," continued Will Simpson, "has the white man solved any problem for us? They ARE the problem. It is them who brought the alcohol that is killing our youth. It is them that exploit them in their inhumane mines, from where they return exhausted, sick and poisoned. It is them who scared the big caribou herds away."

"They will take your son, that's for sure," said Robert. "But not to make him a better man, just to lock him in one of their jails that are places of degradation and despair. And his family will be without a provider. When he returns, he will be full of anger and darkness. His spirit will no longer be with him. We have seen this too often."

Jimmy contemplated silently the five elders gathered around his table, at the dancing light of the fire in the fireplace. Those men, now weak and wrinkled, with gnarled bones and toothless mouths, were the once powerful hunters that mocked him. The same ones who passed by him without watching, vigorously pushing their sleds, feeling happy not to be like him, to have two strong legs, to deserve the girls' glances and to be able to provide for a family.

Those who were now so earnestly advising him, had let him out of many other circles where they boasted their hunting feats around a fire just like this one, but they were not the same and neither was Jimmy. They no longer laughed at him but, ironically, he no longer wanted to belong in their circle. The time of fearing them and being ashamed in front of them was over. Jimmy was now a powerful man. More powerful than they were. In fact most of them, he considered with some contempt, owed him money, for they could not even afford to pay for their groceries or their tobacco.

"You all know that my son does not bear my own blood," he said at last. "But after all, what is blood? To my understanding, it is just a sticky smelly fluid that has nothing to do with the soul. Amorak has grown up as my son and he has been brought up as a Dogrib. I don't believe I have failed him, at least no more than can be expected from a human being. I know he had a difficult childhood before joining our family. We don't talk about it because Amorak has chosen not to and we respect and understand his silence.

We love him as our own child, the same as you love your own. He is the most important thing in the world to us. So I don't understand why you come here today to defend him as if I were his enemy. I will defend my son to death if necessary and I don't need a bunch of old men to teach me how to do it." There was a deep silence in the room and then he continued.

"However there are other people you don't seem to consider worthy of your defense: my daughter-in-law, Cynthia and my grandchildren Edzo and Jiewa. They have been suffering for years the maddened behavior of my son. Perhaps because of my handicap, I have learnt to value the warmth and security of feeling home and I can imagine how terrible it must be for them not to have a place to call home. Finally, my brave granddaughter has spoken up," he roared, raising his chin in defiance. "Should I turn my back to her so that my son can keep on poisoning himself and destroying them? Is this what you call justice?"

The elders considered his words, acknowledging and respecting the anger in them. The sparkling of the fire was, for some minutes, the only voice amongst them.

"At least let us speak to him," said Robert. "We're not totally stupid or merciless. Perhaps we can touch his heart, awaken in him fear and respect. We are his elders after all."

Jimmy skeptically looked at them one by one. "I don't believe my son will respect the elders' circle," he concluded. "I don't believe he respects anything at all. Not even himself. It is very painful for me to admit it, but I believe his spirit abandoned him long ago."

"If you'd only let us try," said Will. "If it doesn't work, if as you say, your son is lost beyond hope and he disrespects our advice, you can always go to the police." He said this last word as though taking it by force from his throat.

"If it doesn't work?" Jimmy roared, punching the table. "You talk as if it was about testing a new trap for martens. If it doesn't work, my grandchildren will keep living in a place of fear and torture."

"And if it works," suggested Sam Moosenose, "your son will still have a chance and your granddaughter will not become an outcast."

Jimmy noticed immediately the veiled threat that laid in the slithering words. He was warning him they would not tolerate his granddaughter's betrayal and they would make her pay for it dearly. If he supported Jiewa, he would be leading her to isolation, to losing her community's respect, her place among her people. He clenched his fists and lowered his gaze, defeated.

Not much more was said in that meeting, but a couple of days later, the elders went, as promised, to see Amorak. He tended to them with the due courtesy as they spoke to him about the importance of the family in their culture and how alcohol kills, and that they would not tolerate his behavior. He had agreed humbly to each statement and once the last of them had left his house, he had battered his wife and children for alerting the community about him. This had been shortly before his untimely death.

Entrusting the problem to the elders had been a mistake, but a mistake made in good faith and Lisa felt bad for throwing salt on Jimmy's open wounds. However, if they only had let her speak, if she had had the chance to say what she thought and what she felt instead of forcing her to apologize for being a woman and for being Inuit. But a lot of 'if onlys' would not give her back her son. She shrugged to dismiss the memories and, between indifference and shiver, she decided not to apologize and she kept on sewing.

Even though the thermometer at the porch marked forty below and Jimmy had not picked up his coat on his way out, he did not feel the cold as he lit a cigarette to calm his nerves and the guilt that was clenching his stomach. With a move of his hand he shooed away the bad thoughts as he exhaled a mouthful of smoke. No. There was no way he could ever have taken part in the incarceration of his own son in one of those dehumanized jails of the whites. Nor in having his granddaughter disowned by the Community. How to make Lisa understand, how to make Jiewa and Edzo understand, how to make even angry Cynthia understand? Was there any way he could be redeemed?

Obviously not, now that Amorak was dead and he had cursed himself for stopping the girl in her first attempt to gather the necessary strength to break free. For not supporting her in her brave challenge to his miserable father and his community. It was as though finally, Jiewa had started to fly and he had cut off her wings. And to what end?

Not only he felt old, but he felt like a vile old man, a coward spreading the example of his cowardice to his own grandchildren. And his wife, for the first time in more than thirty years of marriage, had broken his heart.

"Perhaps now you are starting to understand, you old imbecile," said Lisa from the door, taking him out of his reverie.

"Understand what?" he asked jadedly.

"You are there, feeling sorry for yourself, wallowing in your misery, as if it were all about you. Just like when the elders came to see you, you thought it was about you. Or your legs. Or Amorak, whatever. In fact, all this tragedy is not and has never been about you or your son, but about Jiewa and Cynthia. It is a tragedy of women, like most tragedies," she said and went back into the house, making a point to slam the door noisily.

XIII

Jimmy was not a demanding man. He was normally satisfied with the small routines of his days, the quiet flowing of the seasons, his familiar tasks, his smokes, the warmth of his wife beside him in bed, the visits of his grandchildren, a couple of laughs with friends. Not much. But all of it had gone awry with his son's death. So not only he had to deal with his own grief, but he had stopped feeling familiar in his own skin, unwelcome in his own home and at odds with the memory of his son, whom he could not banish to a shameful corner of his heart, even though he knew he had made so much harm.

He was a Dogrib, a man of his clan. His family was a part of him and he was a part of his family. Only there was no family anymore. Each of them was dealing with anger, resentment, and loss in a different direction. He did not know how to help them or how to help himself. He desperately needed to recover that tough strident family of his, no matter how, and he could not stop thinking of it. He was lost, obsessed like a white man, instead of being present in his works and his environment. He had stopped tending to his business because he could not stand the sympathetic glances that the patrons shot at him. He was of the opinion that drawing people's attention, for the good or for the bad, was never a helpful thing.

One morning, Lisa begged him to go to the store, which he had left under the supervision of his nephew Dolphus, who was no Bill Gates, and the accounts, according to her, were so tangled and orders so delayed that she feared they would go to receivership. Jimmy knew this was pure exaggeration. Of course, Dolphus was not a business genius, but his job was not especially complicated. Lisa's true urgency was to take him out of his house, his pajamas, and his depression, so he agreed unwillingly, somehow relieved that she still cared for him. He cut his face while shaving and got to the store with an improvised toilet paper band-aid.

His sister Adele came to the store that morning and had a loud laugh when she saw him at the other side of the counter.

"That Inuit of yours is becoming a wildcat," she said pointing at the scratch on his face.

"That'll be thirty-five twenty, Adele," he said giving her a sideway look.

"Oh, just add it to my account," Adele said, shaking her hand nonchalantly, as though she did not know that her account had overcome any reasonable limit long ago. "How are Jiewa and Edzo? I keep calling them to visit but there's no way of taking them out of the house. Hermits…"

"You're lucky," Jimmy said. They don't even pick up the phone when I call. They must have a caller identifier, or whatever it is called.

"Is it that bad, brother?" she asked.

"Worse."

"Bring Jiewa a puppy," she suddenly said, lightening up, as though she had had the idea of the century.

"Um… Adele, in case you hadn't noticed, she does have a dog. It doesn't have a name, and it is normally tied up fifty yards from the house, where they feed him every now and then. If it survives this winter, which I doubt, the policemen will shoot it when they see him prowling for food and children in the spring. Why would I deliver another poor beast to the same destiny?"

"No, no, no," she said, laughing, erasing the idea on the air with a playing hand. "I don't mean one of them wolf dogs. I mean a doggie. One of those cute woolly puppies. The girls like Jiewa love them. The other day Oprah was saying that they are very good for people who can't express their feelings and stuff."

"Adele, you watch too much TV," he answered, chuckling.

"Well, say what you want, but it is true that animals soften people's hearts. Remember John Hogan's cockatoo?"

And he had to admit that he did remember John Hogan's cockatoo. John Hogan had been for many years the Town Administrator in Tsiigehtchik. Jimmy and Adele had met him while celebrating Adele's birthday in MacKenzie Lounge, in Yellowknife. It was difficult to miss him, for he was sitting in one of the sofas with a group of friends, one of them being the cockatoo, who laughed like a buccaneer while drinking Corona beer from his master's bottle.

Adele had approached him to meet the exotic bird and immediately fell in love with John Hogan's watery blue eyes. The kind of eyes from John Huston's movies characters, that seem to be laughing and crying at the same time. They ended up sharing the table and the birthday celebration, in the old Yellowknife way, and the cockatoo ended up choosing Adele's lap as a favorite accommodation to drink his beer. She contemplated the bird in awe, occasionally caressing him with admiration and love, like a child contemplating his first Christmas tree. How was that tropical bird possible in the Arctic? The contradiction was beautiful and pungent at the same time yet somehow scary. A rough fifty-something-year-old man protecting an animal that, even in warm weather, would be delicate and vulnerable. A man of the arctic protecting a soap bubble, a circus hallucination, or one of those childhood dreams we never want to wake up from.

Hogan always travelled with his bird. He was too beloved to him to leave him in anybody's care, lest he might not be treated or fed properly, or feel unwelcome. He had lost his wife several years ago at the hands of the inescapable divorce that was the doom of the white men who migrated toward the North with white women. Some of them, with a superhuman adaptation capacity, stayed and slowly built up a life with a forced meaning, or became alcoholics, or embraced religious fanaticism. However, most of them kept travelling southwards under the pretext of visiting family, more and more often and for longer periods of time, until one day they never came back and there was only the bitterness of their ghosts in the long blizzard nights.

Many of these divorced men married native women, thus clashing frontally with a culture that, until then, had been totally alien to them, even If they had been living amidst it for years. Suddenly they could not put up with the caribou meat hanging from the kitchen beams or the very real and overwhelming presence of the whole clan in their lives.

Others, most of them, remained lonely, became alcoholics and acquired the looks of old trees withered by the wind, with long beards, beer bellies, and dirty clothes. Hogan had escaped both destinies by 'adopting' the cockatoo. And the cockatoo had a story that deserved being told, so Hogan told it and they listened without blinking.

As it turned out, the cockatoo had been bought initially by the Tsiigehtchik school because someone thought it was a great idea for children to have such an exotic mascot and because there was some money left from some government funding and everyone agreed they'd rather burn the money than return it to the government. Logical ideas run thin when deadlines for expenses run closer, so someone saw the bird in a pet shop in Edmonton and thought, wouldn't it be great for the kids to share their classroom with the little Australian mate?.

The thing is the school ended up closed. Its turnout was ridiculously low and the handful of children who attended, fell asleep to the lullaby-ish voice of the teachers and the well-adjusted heating of the building. But the cost of that heating was indeed too high for the meager use of the building.

After the closure, nobody wanted to take the cockatoo which ended up at the janitor's home. For him the creature was as bothersome as it was mysterious and useless. Not knowing what to do with it, he gave it to his dealer in exchange for some marijuana. The dealer kept it at home for some time, for it was flamboyant and it really impressed his friends at first. Alas it was too noisy for his wife, who very soon ordered him to get rid of the skinny and aggressive bird that was not even good for soup.

The dealer thought that, anyhow he had to take some profit from the bird. After all he had taken it as payment for a good marijuana delivery, so he had to recover the investment.

One summer afternoon, he took the cage with the cockatoo, covered it with a blanket and walked the streets in search of a buyer. House by house he asked whether anyone would be interested in the prodigious creature from the South, even souther than Edmonton, that brought good luck.

People stared at it in amazement. The children laughed and put their fingers through the bars, only to have them hit by Rocky's powerful grey beak. But nobody saw any sense in owning that shivering bird that was not edible and exhibited a criminal belligerence to anyone approaching him.

By the time when he arrived in the administrator's office, the dealer was tired and fed up, willing to get rid of his burden and go for a drink, so the price of the animal had dropped considerably.

John heard a racket of oooohs and aaaaahs among the employees and he came out of his office to see what the hell was going on. As soon as he saw Rocky and made sure it was not a hallucination, he immediately decided to protect that helpless and almost extraterrestrial creature. So after a quick bargain, he kept Rocky, mostly for humanitarian reasons, although he never suspected Rocky would steal his heart the way he did.

It took some time to get the animal's trust, since all the teasing among hostile strangers had made him a wary and destructive bird. He even attacked John on a couple of occasions, causing considerable wounds. John forgave his friend's fear, he forgave the violent product of fear and he reached the heart of the small enigmatic being that would become his most beloved companion.

"John, this bird was very lucky to find you," Adele had said that night as she gently caressed the bird. He nodded, his liquid blue eyes laughing at the cockatoo that romped happily, sipping beer from Adele's glass and laughing his maddened horselaugh.

"I was also lucky to find him," he said. And he meant it.

John Hogan's cockatoo's memory was a fond one, Jimmy thought that morning at the shop. And although he dismissed Adele, mocking her crazy suggestions, the idea remained there, like a seed germinating slowly in his head and that night, as he had his last cigarette of the day at his porch, it came back to him. The puppy thing might work; for sure it might. And why not? Women on TV—and Jiewa watched a lot of TV—were always hugging puppies and kittens; they must have some power over them.

"There you are. Smoking again," said his wife leaning her head through the door.

"Good observation," he answered. "I was thinking of giving Jiewa a puppy." He dropped the cigarette and squished it with the sole of his boot.

"A puppy?" asked Lisa, astonished. "Your brains are really softening from old age. Don't you see she has her dog more abandoned than hope, always tied away from the house? That is, if it has not been eaten by the wolves as we speak."

"No. I mean one of these puppies on TV, that are good for nothing and sleep all day in front of the fireplace, or jump from lap to lap. Those little thingies you women deem so cute. Oprah says animals soften people's hearts," he said, quoting Adele's speech. Lisa shook her head in disbelief.

"Honestly…" she murmured. "You'd better buy her a bunny," she said as she pushed him softly inside, from where a delicious smell of roasted chicken emerged. "That way they could at least eat it when they've had enough of it."

XIV

"Holy! You've gotten yourself a fag dog," said Cynthia as she opened the door to Jimmy, who had the little white poodle puppy under his arm. Ignoring Jimmy's complaints, Lisa had placed a big pink bow on the puppy's neck that made it look even more preposterous. Jimmy quietly prayed that the neighbours did not see him with the creature in his arms.

Good start, thought Jimmy. He forced a cordial smile. "May I come in?" Cynthia sighed, turned around for the kitchen and left the door ajar. Jimmy entered and closed the door with his foot as he held the puppy with one arm and his crutches with the other one.

In the living room, Jiewa watched TV in a trance. Judging by her position on the sofa, she looked as though she'd fallen there from a great height. She was wearing training pants and an old torn T-shirt. Her greasy hair was tied up in a ponytail. There were two empty chip bags and an empty coke bottle on the carpet nearby. She greeted him with a nod, her gaze still riveted to the TV. Jimmy shook his head in disappointment.

"I brought a surprise," he said in a monotone voice that did not transmit the glee that should rightfully have accompanied the announcement. Jiewa turned around indolently. In Jimmy's mental rehearsal, this was the moment when she jumped up, as though propelled by a spring, and picked up the puppy from his hands, covering him in kisses and little shrieks of pleasure and delight. Instead, she looked at it quietly for some seconds, as though studying it, and then returned to watching TV.

"If you wanted to replace my father, you'd better have gotten me a weasel," she said.

Jimmy cursed between his teeth because the 'fag dog' had cost him eight hundred dollars in Yellowknife, and judging by the enthusiasm with which he had been received by both women, he could foresee he would end up keeping it.

He plopped heavily on the battered sofa where he always sat down and left the puppy on the floor, but the animal started to yell desperately, so he had to put it in his lap, wishing with all his heart that it wouldn't pee. He stared at the dog in silence. Where these animals had come from and the use the whites made of them was a mystery. *White men are truly very alone in this planet,* he thought.

On TV, a bunch of skinny teens talked amongst themselves with a vocabulary and a self-assurance totally beyond their age, rather of forty-something adults, and not even that, since forty-somethings came pretty thick these days. He tried to fix his attention on the show, in order to identify himself with his granddaughter's interests, but those kids, in spite of the astounding colorfulness of their vocabulary and clothing, only spoke crap. They spoke it real fast so that one could not notice it was crap, like 'Omygod! I have absolutely nothing to wear this evening. I'm gonna have to have to visit the mall, anybody's game? I wouldn't like to come across Brandon on my own.' This question gave way to a debate on Brandon and the mall that lasted for several minutes followed by a commercial cut. He looked at Jiewa sideways, to make sure she was really absorbed in that buffoonery. Apparently she was. Jimmy raised his eyebrows in disbelief.

"I've been thinking," he said during the commercials, "that we could use a hand in the store. Lisa has a lot of sewing to do and

I can't come and go all day refilling shelves on my own. Besides Dolphus can't really` cope with the work. Would you be interested? That would mean some extra money for you."

"Whatever," said Jiewa, transfixed by the TV.

Jimmy was quiet as the show came back on. He pretended to be following it, watching Jiewa intensely from the side of his eye, like a hunter stalking a difficult prey he doesn't know how to attack. Teenagers were by nature prickly, but this one had deep wounds and was enveloped in a powerful halo of distrust and anger. However, there was a special connection between them. There had always been. At least until he refused to support her in reporting Amorak to the police.

He expected to have reached her on the night of Amorak's death. He knew that her soul had listened to his feelings. He knew that their spirits had connected, but there was still poison that needed to be purged. He didn't have a clue how to begin.

"Tell me, Jiewa, do you miss him at least a little bit?" he asked with the urgency of a man on death row, feeling the stupidity of the question as he was blurting it out. He braced for the storm that was obviously coming. But storm was better than nothing.

"Miss him!" she exclaimed, glaring at him in disbelief. Her eyes were full of fury, but she finally was looking at him, even though on TV, the skinny girl who had nothing to wear had ended up coming across Brandon at the mall. "Have you lost your fucking mind? What should I miss? When I had to sleep out so that he would not fuck me, or when he hit my brother until he was a shaking sack on the corner?"

"Please, Jiewa…" said Jimmy, raising his palms to appease her, or to protect himself against the crude images. "Respect a father's pain."

"And how, eh? How could I know about a father's pain when I never had one? And, umm… speaking of pain, did you give a shit about *my* pain? Now, shut the fuck up. I'm missing my favorite show."

"And yet there has to be something," Jimmy insisted with a suicidal vehemence, in spite of the pain, in spite of the blood galloping in his ears. "Something he did right at some point in your lives. Even if it was only to tell funny jokes or sing songs to you as a baby, or make wooden toys for you guys. *Something*."

"Nothing!" she bellowed with red hot rage lighting up her eyes. "I don't miss absolutely nothing! And there was nothing he did right, unless you count making us all miserable. That he did fucking well. And now that you ask, I'm very happy he died. I hope he suffered lots. Too bad he was not eaten alive by the wolves. And now piss off and let me watch my show, you old fart!"

Jimmy took some deep breaths as he considered her angry words, amazed he himself hadn't dropped dead from a heart attack. He remembered the respect he was taught to give his elders. And what a business he had done, for now that the elder was he, the tradition was lost and this brat treated him like garbage.

Once his heart regained its regular beat, he stood up slowly, put the puppy on the floor, took his crutches, walked to his granddaughter. For the first time in his life, he gave her a smack on the face, the kind that leaves a red handprint for several minutes. She uttered a short scream, half startled, half angry. She put her hand to her cheek, gazing at him incredulously as though seeing him under a new light. There was nothing else to say. The grandfather left the house without saying goodbye. He was thankful for the chilly evening air on his tired flushed face. He breathed in repeatedly, deeply, greedily, leaning against the door. "I'm too old for this stuff," he thought, placing his rough hand on his chest, trying to soothe his heart that was beating like a wild bird in a cage.

As he slowly worked his way through the snow towards his truck parked by the house, he heard what sounded like a sudden strong beating of wings behind him, accompanied by some shrill yelps. He turned around, shocked, expecting to find his grand-daughter running to him in anger, ready to return the smack to him, which to be honest, would not have surprised him in the least. But what he saw was a massive arctic owl lifting the puppy in its claws. The horrifying scene left him in suspense for a moment. He had not even noticed the puppy had followed him outside of the house. In a hunter's reflex, he threw one of his crutches to the bird, but even though he hit it, it did not let go of the prey and after a brief oscillation in its trajectory, it flew away heavily to the purple twilight sky, the pink bow waving goodbye, like a grotesque birthday streamer.

Jimmy remained sitting on the snow, panting, with frustration tears in his eyes. "There goes an eight hundred dollar supper," he said, furious, as he crept toward his other crutch.

XV

"The results of your tests seem to be fine, but you don't look good, Jimmy. Is something wrong?" said the doctor without raising his eyes from a form in Jimmy's already bulky file where he was scribbling something hastily. Jimmy waited patiently for him to finish writing, but judging by the time he was taking, he seemed to be writing his own memories on that paper. The doctor finally raised his eyes and threw him an inquisitive look. "And?" he urged him.

"And? What?" asked Jimmy, annoyed.

"Well, I was asking…"

"I know what you were asking, seeing as so far I'm not deaf. Yet. You were asking me a question you normally make to a friend, looking in his eyes, when you have the time to listen opening your heart. Now. Are you looking at me in the eye? Are you my friend? Do you have the time to listen with an open heart?"

The doctor stared at him, speechless, with only one eyebrow up, which was a weird thing to do.

"Then why the hell do you ask?" Jimmy said, and without waiting for an answer, he stood up leaning on his crutches and left the room.

On his way home he reproached himself for being rude to the doctor. After all he was just following the cardboard courtesy rules of the whites. Anyway, even though he still thought he was a bit of a pompous imbecile, he promised himself to send some caribou ribs to his home as an apology. Indeed the man was right. He did not feel well at all. He could not sleep at night and spent his days from one sofa to the other, without shaving or showering, just snoozing and wandering through the house like a zombie in his pajamas, zapping the TV without really watching or listening to anything on it, just to shoo away the nightmares in which his son burnt in hell, or Jimmy asked people in the community and nobody had ever heard of him. But worst of all were those times when he dreamed Amorak was still alive and he awoke to the realization that he was not. He wondered if Lisa had the same nightmares but he never dared to ask. He did not want to broaden the range of themes for his nightly horrors.

His days passed in the grey zone of those who live without enthusiasm, and it was in that grey zone that death chose its prey. He was in no hurry to die, at least not before he fixed up his family. If fixing was possible at all, that was.

Back at home from the health center, he went to the kitchen to make himself a cup of tea. The snow water container was empty. He hit it against the counter, annoyed. No elder of Nogha Ti could drink tea made with chlorinated water from the water plant. They could not get used to the taste, which they considered poisonous. They gathered virgin snow instead and let it melt to drink and make tea.

Jimmy filled the kettle with tap water, put it on the stove and sat at a kitchen chair to wait for the whistle, as he grimly considered his situation and his feelings. After brewing his tea, he went to the living room with his steaming mug and slumped on the sofa. He was tempted to take a couple of the pain killers the doctor prescribed him regularly, which he kept stashing in the bathroom cabinet, but he discarded the idea, because he did not believe the soul pain could be medicated.

His living room was the safest and quietest place in the world for him, where nothing unexpected could happen, where everything was predictable, familiar and friendly. At least until some weeks ago, when his entire world fell apart. He liked the old sofas, tamed to their shapes. The framed pictures covering the walls, his wife's beautiful sewing box, the pile of sewing orders beside it that smelled of chicory and smoke. The white lace curtains that sifted the daylight into a relaxing luminescence that licked the familiar objects' profiles. The silence was familiar too; the small noises of the pipes, the faraway scream of a kid playing outside, the muffled sound of a ski-doo, the singing of a raven claiming its territory.

He was now seated on the corner, right by the wooden desk where he did his accounting, where the small brown phone book tucked into the second drawer that had been on his mind for the latest days, laid untouched. He looked warily at the desk, as if it were somehow haunted, and wasn't it after all? He approached the mug to his mouth, but immediately the chlorine smell touched the inside of his nose like an acid. He lowered the mug, grimacing, but kept turning it in his hands, trying to look away from the desk. He turned on the TV and zapped nervously without seeing or listening to anything. He turned the TV off and reclined on the sofa, thinking that maybe he could have a snooze and forget about the brown phone book. The old leather phone book with dog-eared pages that lay in the second drawer of the desk.

The phone book with Veronique's number in it. The actual one, the one in Vancouver. She had given it to him before leaving Yellowknife and he had treasured it throughout the years, making sure it did not change, making sure he did not let go of this frail umbilical cord, a few figures that linked him to his white woman.

His Veronique. Not that he had ever called her. Not for Christmas and not for her birthday. Neither had she. It was not necessary. He just wanted to keep her number. It would be too scary not to.

One night he had had a very vivid dream of her. He awoke in the middle of the night covered in sweat, and the very next morning, he had to check with the telephone company that the number had not changed. And he kept checking now and then. It was a futile exercise, because he had not talked to her or seen her ever since she left Yellowknife, and that was more than forty years ago. It was just he could not let her go completely.

He did not know why he felt the urge to call her now. He had once heard that old men, whilst having short term forgetfulness, have very clear memories from long ago. Maybe it was just that, a trick from his wasted brain. Or perhaps he needed to summon a time in his life when everything had been easy, a time of light, of passion, of laughter. Maybe Veronique's voice could summon some incantation that helped him stand up and face his son's death and moreover, his son's life. They would not be two strangers on the phone, this he knew, because they had been much more than lovers; they had been soul mates, and that kind of bond never wanes.

He also knew she had never been one to demand a smart conversation from her partners. You did not even have to be coherent or socially acceptable to talk to her and get the spark in her eyes and her musical laughter to accompany your nonsense. This was a very comforting personality trace, especially now, when he needed to call her quietly and talk to her without coordination or structure, about his pain and confusion. Perhaps even cry. Maybe solve this crazy puzzle together.

What stopped him and made his hands sweat was how to explain this need to Lisa. The last thing he wanted was to hurt her, and God knew she had had her share of pain lately. And yet he would have to explain it to her, or he would feel like a miserable coward traitor.

Would not the phone call be an infidelity on itself? It probably would, he considered, nodding. But the memory of Veronique's soothing singing voice was smoothly cuddling into his heart and the possibility of that disloyal phone call was becoming an inexorable destiny.

He took a swig of the infamous chlorinated tea, which made him grimace in revulsion. He went to the kitchen and dropped it in the sink, refilling the mug with scotch. Now that was a fluid the whites could make with some art. He returned to the living room and made his way to the desk. He opened the dreaded and desired second drawer, took the old phone book that had been dormant for so many years and sat on the sofa again.

He spent a while there feeling very stupid, whisky in one hand, phone book in the other. Nerves clutching his stomach, hands sweating. Finally he took a big swig of whisky, opened the book and dialed Veronique's number in Vancouver. A man's voice answered after three rings. This did not shock Jimmy, since he had always assumed she would get married again.

"Good morning. Can I speak with Veronique Leduc?" he asked, rubbing his hand on his thigh to wipe the sweat. A long silence came back from the line.

"May I ask who is calling her?" the voice finally responded.

"This is Jimmy Whitefox. An old friend from the Northwest Territories." Silence followed again.

"This is Mason Leduc," said the man in Vancouver at last. "I am Veronique's son. I'm sorry to inform you that she passed away two years ago," he said awkwardly. Jimmy felt as if he had just received a punch on the stomach. He would never have anticipated that she might be dead. She who was the expression of life itself. How come he had not felt her death, when it was such a gigantic death? How could he have remembered her alive and young for two years when she was dead? How could he have missed the absence of such a vital and powerful spirit, a spirit that was like a twenty thousand caribou herd running over a frozen lake? A spirit that was so intimate to him?

"Hmm... Mr. Whitefox?" the voice questioned warmly on the phone. "Are you still there?" Jimmy hung up the phone, unable to say a word.

He stood up like a robot, put on his parka and boots and went out to the lake with the ski-doo and the toboggan to gather some snow for tea. He was in a daze, lifeless, as the machine crossed the hard surface of the lake; white and infinite like the emptiness he felt inside. Finally he stopped, far enough from the village that the houses looked like a toy town. He got the shovel and started to fill the toboggan with unsoiled snow. When he had enough, he removed his hood, raised his head to the intense arctic blue sky, inhaling the chilly air until his lungs hurt and in the merciless white solitude of the lake, he sat on the machine and started to cry. His cry rose slowly until it became a scream and he felt that his old heart was tearing apart.

XVI

Jimmy tried to accommodate his sore legs in the little room in the twin otter seat. He looked through the window at the white blanket of the tundra, trying to spy with hunter's eyes, caribou tracks, or a pack of wolves startled by the plane's roar. It was already early spring and life began to reawaken with the thawing of the snow. The colors were beginning to blossom after the long hermetic cold season. For the first time, he had not felt the transition in his body. His heart was stagnant, disconnected from the environment, like the heart of a white man. This old heart, however, felt lighter in flight, because he had never got over the beauty and amazement of flying. He wondered why he had never considered becoming a bush pilot. Even now, numbed and exhausted from pain, he felt like a child in the clouds.

He had planned this flight to Kugluktuk partly to try to reach an armistice with the memory of his son and partly to escape the oppressive hostility that seemed to close around him like a shroud. Weeks kept passing slowly in the lethargy of mourning that was slowly settling into their lives, like an unwanted guest one cannot kick out and is always there, occupying the best sofa and lazily smearing everything with its stench. Perhaps that was the trick, Jimmy thought. Since the pain of a son's death cannot be cured, maybe the best was to give it space and let it howl until one got used to the noise.

And yet it was not easy. Jimmy discovered that memories were like soldiers that gained rank with years; the older ones were the most painful ones. The first years with Amorak, his first smiles when he discovered that life could be beautiful, his proud face when they hunted their first rabbit together, Christmas mornings, fishing days, sharing a man-to-man silence over the mirror of the lake. All those things that had once built up his modest day-to-day happiness had now become mortal enemies that jumped out unexpectedly at a certain smell, or song, or picture.

Lisa kept sewing in silence like Penelope, only she didn't undo her work—she was smarter—radiating a forced serenity from her corner. It seemed as though she were sewing her own heart with the same coordination and discipline she used for her charges. Sometimes he looked at her for long periods of time, trying to unveil her secret, and he shook his head in disapproval. He knew her silence was a reproach, a reminder that he needed to bring her back her grandchildren. And probably that was the trick; to try again and again. To go to the house where he was so much despised, knock on the door and be humiliated one hundred times until they gave up, or until he had a heart attack, or one of those long-named strokes that habitually annihilate elders.

It was not that he feared being humiliated. At his age he had finally conquered his honor and it belonged to him only. No, it was not a question of pride, but of fear. He dreaded that family that reminded him with their mere presence that his son was unworthy of being loved or mourned. Had he been a thief or a murderer, he would have been forgiven. In cases even admired. But abusing a child made of a man a worthless spoil underserving of respect. Jimmy understood this, but it could not keep him from loving his son and from cherishing his memory. The same memory that was unspeakable doom in his daughter-in-law's home. So he stayed away.

Up in the air he was feeling somehow like a fugitive, knowing it was cowardly to leave Lisa in the same trouble he was escaping from, but the fact was, she was also angry at him. Angry for not having been able to speak her mind in that goddamned elders meeting that decided her son's fate. Angry because she felt that her son and her family and been stolen from her by those arrogant elders who didn't even bother looking at her—and this included Jimmy himself. And she was also irritated about the incident with the puppy. It seemed she had really warmed up to the little poodle and since she was certain the poor thing would be rejected by Cynthia, her generous heart had already adopted him. She had even given him a little Inuit name that Jimmy made a point not to ever learn. In the last morning of the puppy's short life, she had been feeding him bread soaked in milk, watching him in awe lick the food with his tiny pink tongue.

Jimmy noted in his mind to tell Adele, without economizing vocabulary, where she could put her Oprah advice the next time.

The lights of Kugluktuk's humble airport lit automatically as the instruments detected the airplane, marking an indigo path for landing over the pressed white snow. The aircraft landed softly and left the passengers by the white hangar that was the airport. Of course nobody awaited him, and he was carrying no luggage, so he started to walk feeling the freedom of lightness.

There was now a hotel where Old McNally's ratty bar used to be. He came in to have a sandwich and a soup. After he paid, he went outside and started working on the difficult task he had come here for.

The village had changed so much that it seemed impossible to locate the log cabin that, most likely, no longer existed. After a long walk, he found what he thought was the place, but just as he had foreseen, instead of the poor cabin where Amorak had spent his early childhood, there was now an impersonal grey trailer home. Jimmy stood there, like a mouse at the beginning of a maze.

But it was normal. After all, what had he come back to this place for? Did he know? After a while, he knocked on the neighbour's door. An obese Inuit with walrus mustache and amber eyes opened the door.

"Can I help you?" he asked, panting, as if the way to the door had been an obstacle race.

"Good afternoon," said Jimmy removing his beaver hat. "You don't know me. I have come from Nogha Ti to learn about the family who used to live in the cabin," he said pointing at the space now occupied by the trailer. The man did not follow his pointing hand, but stared at him intensely.

"I know you," he said at last. "You are the Dogrib that took the kid away." His stare moved from impertinence to interest. He moved his heavy body from the doorway and invited him in. "Come on in; let's have a drink to celebrate."

"I'm afraid there's not much to celebrate," said Jimmy shaking the snow from his boots as he entered.

"Doesn't matter. Even the company of a Dogrib ripper is better than drinking alone. We'll drink," he said good-humoredly, referring to the bloody battles of their ancestors.

"Why, thank you, friggin' seal snatcher," Jimmy said as he left his boots by the door and entered the kitchen. The Inuit threw his head back and launched a powerful laugh that shook his big belly. He pointed at a chair by the kitchen table and Jimmy sat down, propping his crutches against the wall. The Inuit took out a bottle and two glasses from an alcove and put them on the table. Then he filled both glasses up to the rim and sat heavily in front of Jimmy.

"By the way, my name is Archie. Yours?"

"Jimmy Whitefox."

"Right on," Archie snorted, pointing at Jimmy's white hair. "How's the boy? Well, he's no boy anymore, he must be, what? Forty-something?"

"He's dead," Jimmy answered, and Archie nodded thoughtfully, looking into his glass.

"And what are you here for?"

"What?" Jimmy asked, startled from the daze he always fell into after informing someone of his son's death.

"Amorak's family," Archie said. "You said you wanted to know about them. What is it you need to know? Not that there's much to tell, anyway."

Jimmy closed his eyes and squeezed them with his index and thumb, attempting to stop what promised to be the headache of the century. "I want to know if they were good to Amorak," he said bluntly.

"I don't understand," Archie said, incredulous. "You're very far away from your home, Dogrib. Why do you come here if the man is dead? Are you chasing ghosts like the white men?"

"Maybe," Jimmy admitted, taking a gulp from his glass of whisky.

Archie sighed heavily and buried his face between his meaty hands. "Okay," he agreed. "I'm gonna tell you what I know and it's not pretty, Dogrib. The mom you only met as a cadaver but I'll say that she wasn't much different as a living body. Always drunk she was. There was never food or firewood in that house. It all went into drinking. Every now and then we'd bring them wood or dried fish, whatever we had for ourselves. The father came very seldom, to sell seal skins on the Bay. He always brought many," he said frowning. "The motherfucker was a good hunter. I never got so many. Anyway. Whenever he came, he always stayed for some days in his cabin. He brought flour, sugar, nails and what not. He was nasty and violent, always looking for a fight where there was none to be had, so nobody around here was happy to see him. Amorak the least of all. As soon as he got a whiff of his presence he disappeared and survived sleeping on our kitchen floor or at somebody else's home, and feeding on leftovers or dry fish." Archie took a gulp of his whisky and continued.

"But sometimes he could not escape on time, the poor bloke. Then we heard him scream and cry at night and our hearts went out to him but nobody dared to confront the man."

Jimmy felt a cramp of pain and hatred in his stomach and took a long swig of the beverage to settle down. The Inuit noticed and he shrugged slightly, as though apologizing.

"The man came back after his wife's death. That would be around one year after your left with the kid," Archie continued, turning the glass in his hand. "He stood there, looking at the empty cabin. He had lost one eye, but he had the same deadly expression on his face. Some of us came out to explain to him what had happened. He made a face when we told him it was a Dogrib who had taken his child, but after chewing the thing for a while, he must have decided that it was better that way. You see, he had made another family in Tuktoyaktuk and one more mouth to feed did not seem convenient to him. Of the dead woman he said nothing, as if she had never existed, let alone been his wife."

Archie stood up with a burp, took two dry caribou strips from the ceiling beams, gave one to Jimmy and started to chew his own. They both remained in silence for a while as they ruminated over the salty meat and the past.

"Hey, the kid was lucky to go with you. Otherwise he would have ended up dead, or worse, living with his father. Why can't you be happy about this instead of digging into the dead's miseries, Dogrib?"

Jimmy stared at him openly for a long moment, studying him as a human being, as a hunter and as a drinker. Then he decided to tell him everything. The whole story, without keeping anything in the dark. How Amorak had failed his family, how he had become a violent alcoholic and how—and this was the most difficult part to tell—he had abused his own daughter, and Jimmy had not had the guts to support her when she tried to fight back.

Archie listened, nodding, his slanted eyes clouded to give the story the full strength of his imagination. When Jimmy had finished, he kept silence for some minutes, in case he had something else to say, and then he sighed.

"Eh, what do you want?" he said shrugging his powerful shoulders in a movement that shook his whole stomach. "One's got to do what one's got to do. You can help people but then people take their own ways and your help has no bearing in that. When these hands were still useful," he said raising them in front of his face and looking at them with melancholy, as though they did no longer belong to him, "before becoming a useless fat elder, I was a seal hunter. Way back when they were hunted in the traditional Inuit way. We cut a hole on the ice, over the sea. We covered the hole with a dome of snow. In this dome we made a tiny hole, in front of which we put a tripod made of three seal hairs. Then you had to stand by the hole, over a bear skin, so that your legs did not freeze, bending over your waist as much as possible to be able to watch the tripod, which would quiver when the seals came out of the hole to breath. And you had to be quiet like an inuksuk because if the seals felt your presence they would not use your hole. Sometimes you had to remain in this position for days, never taking your eyes off the small tripod. When the animals came out, the air they breathed made the hairs move and then you threw your harpoon, hoping to be able to hook the seal out of the ice.

"Sometimes you spent days without hunting, frozen and starved, wondering how your family would be coping. In these occasions, when you finally hooked a seal, you had to fight for it with your own dogs that became hungry beasts ready to kill for the meat. In more than one occasion I have had to kill a good dog in a fight," he said with his gaze lost in the remembrance of those animals. "A seal kept my family fed for almost a week. We ate everything, the fat, the blood, the bowels, the marrow. We made coats, mitts and mukluks with their skins.

"And yet sometimes I had to come back home empty-handed, exhausted and numb from exposure, more dead than alive. Empty-handed, see?" he emphasized, producing his hands as a proof. "With nothing to feed my family. You understand, Dogrib? I've buried three children along the way. And would you blame me for failing them, for not being able to provide sometimes? I don't think so, Jimmy, because you are a hunter like me. You know about the eternal winters, the black nights, hunger, the fancy migration of the game. You know that sometimes, even when you do your best and when you lay your snares in the right places, and cover your ice holes to perfection, you go empty-handed."

Archie shrugged again, the palms of his hands upwards. "Now I eat food that I take from cans," he said laughing. "So none of this has sense other than for two old geezers like us that should have gone to the hole in the snow many years ago. But here we are, thanks to the pale faces' obsession for people not to die. And I don't complain, Dogrib. Now I have a home to hang my coat. Back then I didn't have no home and I had to risk my life to get me a coat."

The men kept silent for a while, letting the ghosts of their hunting days dance around the warm kitchen.

"Amorak was a vicious man," Jimmy said, refilling his glass and his friend's. "An alcoholic, a monster. In the end, his spirit was no longer with him. And yet I can't and I don't know if I even want to stop loving him," he confessed.

"Shit! No kiddin'!" snorted the Inuit. "If one could only love the good ones…"

XVII

Seeing as what with the drinking and the conversation Jimmy had missed the evening flight, Archie offered him to overnight at his home. Jimmy asked, mockingly, if he would have to sleep on the kitchen floor, like Amorak used to do as a kid. The Inuit laughed heartily at that.

"That was when the house was full of children," he explained. "One of the privileges of old age is that one has lots of guest rooms."

"Yeah," Jimmy agreed laughing, too. "The problem is that when you get old you don't get as many guests."

It was a nice surprise, though, to check that, against all odds, the guest room was clean and cozy. There must be a Mrs. Archie somewhere, even though he had not met her, because he could not imagine Archie carefully making a bed with his greasy claws. He turned in eagerly, since the day had been exhausting, and for the first time in months, he slept uninterrupted for twelve hours, without dreams or uneasiness. He did not even wake up to go to the bathroom.

The next morning the smell of bacon and coffee awoke him and he went to meet Archie in the kitchen. They ate their breakfast engaged in a good-humored chat and then, before Jimmy left, Archie gave him some sealskin mukluks.

"Made by my wife," he explained. "Too bad that she didn't realize that my legs are now much fatter than that. Maybe it's because she never wants to see me naked anymore."

"I don't blame her," said Jimmy and they both laughed and hugged each other before parting.

Jimmy took two flights to Nogha Ti and once there, he drove home in the store truck which he had left parked at the airport. As he was arriving home, he saw his friend Jack Bearclaw sitting on the bench at his porch.

Bearclaw was some years older than him. Skinny, small, frail, with thick glasses that magnified his eyes and a permanent peaceful smile on his face. Jimmy was happy to see him there, and he wondered why they had spent years without visiting each other. Old age, he thought, muffles passions, both the good ones and the bad ones. Friendship turns into a contact between souls, but no longer between bodies. The bodies are too busy resting.

Jack nodded as he saw him approach, accepting his image such as he had expected to find it. They hugged by the door, without needing to say any words. Jimmy invited him in and prepared some snow tea. As soon as they were comfortably settled on the sofas with their tea mugs, Jimmy knew that Jack had come to tell him something important, so he kept quiet until his friend decided to speak.

"It wasn't bad the way we used to live way back when, eh?" he said smiling, the steam from the mug making his glasses foggy. "I miss the hunting, the life in the bush, the freedom. Although maybe what I really miss is youth itself," Jack chuckled, sipping his tea noisily. "I don't even remember the last time I was with a woman, and it's strange because normally spring got me with this fire inside, you know. But not anymore. My body does not seem to notice spring. At least not down there."

"Oh, yeah, the fire," nodded Jimmy with a melancholy smile and made himself a mental note to make love to his wife more often.

"I just came from Rae Lakes, from my daughter's house," Jack said. "I don't fly there anymore. Even though the Band would pay my ticket. I'd rather go by truck. There is always someone willing to take me there. It's a whole day drive on that difficult track, and you bounce so much you think you will never find your ass again. I like to watch by the window, see the tracks on the snow and guess if they are from a caribou or a wolf, a fox, a wolverine. Even sometimes I make them stop to smell the air if I feel the prey is near. Just for the sake of smelling it, because I know I will never see myself running knife in hand to get the meat, or feel the dogs' excitement at the smell of the blood after days of hunger, the warmth of the still beating meat." He shrugged with a sad smile. "You see, that's all I have left from my days as a hunter. The smell. From women, not even that. And yet I'm pretty sure I was in a relationship with a woman a few years ago," he squinted through his thick glasses, "but, can you believe I don't remember who she was?"

"Better like that, Jack," Jimmy said fondly. "She was Andy Thompson's wife."

"Ah, but of course!" chuckled Jack. "I already knew, old ass. Just wanted to see if you did." They both laughed and then sat in silence, remembering the generous curves and flirtatious smile of the lady in question. Finally, Jack cleared his throat and Jimmy knew that the moment to reveal the purpose of his visit had arrived.

"Jimmy, did you ever see the Bushman?" asked Jack with a serious expression on his face.

"Holy Christ, Jack!" Jimmy exclaimed. "Have they increased your arthritis medication?"

"I can't say I saw it because I never dared to look at it, but it was behind me once, all right. And I still can feel a cold shiver when I remember it," Jack said, ignoring his friend's sarcastic comment. Jimmy tried to scrutinize him for a possible prank, but this was no prank at all. The man was dead serious.

"Well, I have never seen the Bushman, Jack. To tell you the truth, I always thought it was just a legend."

Jack nodded slowly. "Well, your grandchildren seem to have seen it," he said scrutinizing him.

"My grandchildren! Are they okay? What's happened?"

"Easy, Jimmy," Jack said with a smile. "Everything's fine. It's just…You know the water treatment plant they started to build some weeks ago by the lakeshore?" Jimmy nodded briskly, impatient. "Well. It happens that, as they were digging the pits for the tanks, they took out a very fine kind of gravel and Tom, the Administrator, decided to spread it in several crossings in town, to avoid muddy places in our poor unpaved roads come the thaw, in a couple of weeks. He also spread it over the baseball field. All over the place, man."

"Well, it makes sense, doesn't it," said Jimmy.

"Some days later," Jack said, "the Chief and some elders, me being one of them, came to see Tom in his office to complain about what he had done." Jack chuckled again. "The poor bloke could not understand why, for all he had done was spread some nice fine gravel to avoid mud on the streets. And for free, for that matter. 'You don't understand,' Chief Robert said. 'That gravel is polluted.' For a brief moment, Tom was petrified at the idea that he might have built a water treatment plant on a polluted site. Then he relaxed and explained that a team of specialists had come to test the soil and the water and there was no trace of pollution in either. There were no factories around the lake and the waste water was poured far away in a lagoon. The lake water is so clear one can even take a glass right from it and drink. He even produced a file with the report to prove this." Jack giggled again.

"Robert shook his head, tossing impatiently the report on Tom's table. 'You don't understand,' he said, exasperated. 'It's not that kind of pollution. It's the Bushman.' A murmur of disapproval filled the office, for many think you're not supposed to mention that name. 'Jimmy Whitefox's grandchildren saw the Bushman on the grounds of the water plant and now that you have spread that gravel all over town, it can come anytime and take any of us away forever. Oh my God, how could you do it?' he moaned, and the rest of the elders followed suit."

"Wait a moment, was he talking about Jiewa and Edzo?" Jimmy cut in. Jack nodded and went on with his recount.

"The Administrator was speechless. 'The Bushman,' he repeated bleakly in disbelief. 'Who's that? Some kind of poacher?' he asked." At this, both Jimmy and Jack laughed together for a good while. Then Jack continued.

"'No, no!' screamed Robert, pissed off by his incomprehension. 'The Bushman,' he explained patiently, 'is what you would call a Sasquatch, but not quite. It is twice as big as a man, and it has been living in the bush for much longer than us. It is definitely bad news. It is attracted by people who have some kind of wisdom or magic, then it stalks that person until it finally takes him, or her, away forever. We are somehow protected in our settlements since it prowls around in the wilderness, which is its home. The Bushman used to walk on the lakeshore, just where your water plant is being built. Jiewa and Edzo saw it and they were so scared they did not dare to go out for a week.

"'Now you have taken its gravel all over town. Now the Bushman can walk freely by our streets and take away any man it fancies. You must remove that gravel!' Robert ordered firmly. Bill nodded sternly, and said, 'Nah'Gaa,' the Dogrib name of the Bushman, to make Tom understand, but it did not help.

"Freddy then instructed that the gravel needed to be removed and buried. Robert translated this into English, nodding profusely as Tom listened, horrified. 'This is the only way to prevent the Bushman from coming back.'

"Tom smiled at us in disbelief, as though we came out of a bad fish dream. 'Robert, that's more than fifty truckloads of gravel we're talking about. Good gravel that will avoid mud in the main intersections. We are in the middle of the thaw and this will keep our town from becoming a swamp like it does every spring.'

"'We must start at once, Tom,' Robert cut in. 'We are all in danger. Maybe even you.' Hadn't it been for our grave expressions and the fact that he had been working for more than six years in Nogha Ti, he would have thought we were playing a prank on him and we would burst into laughter at any moment. But that didn't happen.

"Tom shifted into his *serious-man-who-means-business* expression. I bet my ass that for a moment, he would have liked to kick us all out of his office with our Bushman stories, for he was there to work on *real* things, and he had a lot of real problems to deal with, by the way. If we thought he would use four men and two or three weeks' salary in shoveling the gravel back into the trucks and burying it, we must be hallucinating, or had no idea about community management, or about the extent of the white government's generosity when it came to eccentricities like that.

"But he said nothing of the sort. He took his time, like a Dogrib would. He studied us in silence for a long moment, one by one. He looked very tired when he said, 'Well, after all, it is your land, your gravel, your mud. Who am I to decide?' We all stayed in silence, admiring his acceptance.

"'But how the hell am I going to justify this work to the auditors back in Yellowknife?' he asked mostly to himself, still resisting the idea a little bit. Robert, who has already had some spiky encounters with the Administration, remained pensive for a moment. 'Let's gather a meeting with Council and elders,' he said at last, 'then we can decide what to do.' All the important elders were already there except you, so here I am, to bring you along. And you arrived right on time."

XVIII

Tom opened the meeting room doors with his keys and everyone followed him inside in silence. Jimmy's grandchildren sat down on the floor, as the elders solemnly took their places at the padded green chairs around the big oval table.

Tom asked Aileen, his secretary, to call the interpreter, since most elders did not speak English.

"Don't bother. He was gambling and drinking last night until late, so he won't answer the phone," said Chief Robert. Tom decided not to ask how he knew. "Matt, you go fetch him," said Robert to one of the onlookers who were gathering in the room. Matt agreed grudgingly and left the building.

As they waited for the interpreter, the elders ordered snow tea and cookies, but when half an hour later the interpreter had not yet arrived, they decided to send Aileen to the store to get some hamburgers and pop. At that moment, Jack and Jimmy entered the meeting room with grave expressions and took their seats around the table. Jimmy could not have sworn it, but he thought he saw his grandchildren's faces cheer up as they saw him.

In anticipation of the possibility that the meeting might, as usual, develop into a banquet, there were many in attendance. Some people were seated on the floor and some were even watching from the door. Just as most anticipated, someone asked the women to make a caribou stew and bannock for the occasion. The suggestion received a unanimous murmur of approval.

Tom had accepted there would be no more office job for the day. It would be an intolerable disrespect to stand up from a meeting with elders and go back to his boring although urgent financial statements. The guys were finishing their hamburgers when Matt arrived, dragging the interpreter to the meeting room, and then closed the door behind him, as if to prevent him from escaping.

The interpreter looked horrible. His eyes were two red slits that the man tried to keep as closed as possible to guard them from the painful light. His breath was probably flammable and his movements were clumsy and slow. He greeted the crowd vaguely and sat in his habitual place, right beside Tom. Aileen brought him a cup of coffee which she put noisily on the table in front of him.

The Chief then stood up for the opening prayer and they all did the same, with their eyes closed and their heads reverently bowed.

He explained the facts to the newcomers in full detail and solemnity. They all kept silence as the elders reflected on what to say, which was their custom, so that their words followed their thoughts and not the opposite. This way they solved problems instead of cultivating egos.

"I want my grandchildren to speak," Jimmy said, breaking the silence. "It was them who saw the Nah'Gaa by the lake." The kids looked at each other and it was Jiewa who stood up to explain.

"It was one morning, two winters ago. My brother and I were having breakfast at the kitchen. It must be around eight, but since it was January, it would still be dark for some hours. You could hardly see anything through the window that looked into the lake, but I was looking anyway. I don't know why. I guess I was looking at myself?" she explained, blushing. "Then I saw something moving outside. First I turned around, thinking it was my brother's reflection on the glass. But he was not moving. He was at the corner, heating up something in the microwave, so it could not have been him. An animal, I thought. But a hell of a big one—sorry—" she apologized for swearing in front of the elders.

"Anyway, I stuck my face to the window and put my hands around my face to see better in case it was a wolverine that came to attack the dog. Then I saw it standing there, on the snow by the lake, looking at me from the dark night, its eyes full of hate. I have never seen so much hate in anybody's eyes. I screamed and got away from the window, scaring my brother, who spilled the milk."

"Yeah, did she ever scream…" Edzo corroborated, eliciting discreet chuckles in the room. "At first that made me angry and I shouted, 'Are you… silly?' seeing as she had made me spill the milk. I looked over at her and, man, was she ever pale, with big open eyes. I asked several times 'Whassup, whassup?' but she was paralyzed. Finally she raised her arm and she pointed at the window. I went there and looked outside as she had done, with my face stuck to the glass. And there was that… being, I don't know what to call it. I still get goose bumps when I remember," he said, rubbing his arms. "But Jiewa is right, he looked with a kind of hate that was not normal. Like… you can't imagine anyone hating like that, you know?"

"We thought it would come for us," he continued, "but for some reason it could not come any closer. Mom says it's cause we have an image of the Virgin by the door and the priest says that the Holy Virgin is very powerful…" He carefully chose his words, shuffling his weight from one leg to the other. "But I think the creature was also, I dunno, kinda stuck in the lakeshore, that he could not come any closer, you know?"

"After that we spent several days without leaving the house," Jiewa continued. "And even now we don't dare to look through the kitchen window, especially at night, because that being sometimes comes back and it stays there looking. He has such hate in his eyes that it makes us shiver deep in our bones. We mostly try to ignore it, lest he makes up his mind to come to the house and kill us, Holy Virgin and all. When we feel it's around, we leave the kitchen slowly, as if we hadn't seen it, and we go to the living room and pray.

After some minutes of reflection, Jack Bearclaw spoke. "I came across it once, many years ago. It was spring. Early spring. I had been checking my snares and I had lingered for too long, so I was getting ready to cook the rabbit I had caught and sleep in a leanto, when suddenly I felt it come through the bush, at my back. It was as the kids say," he nodded, pointing at them with his chin. "It makes your spine shiver so much that it hurts and feels like you are going to freeze. I never thought it might be a bear. I knew from the get go that it was the Nah'Gaa, so I did not want to turn around, because I knew if I did I would die instantly. Don't ask me why, but I knew. It came closer without trying to silence its steps on the bush, until it was right behind me. So close I could feel its heavy breath on the nape of my neck. It sounded like a bear's breath but not quite. It had a kind of human feel, but not quite either. I wouldn't know how to describe it."

"I closed my eyes very tight, because I didn't want to see it before dying. Then it circled me and stood in front of me, but I did not open my eyes. I closed them even tighter. The dogs were quiet. So quiet at some point I thought they might be dead. You could hear no birds, no breeze in the trees. Nothing. More quiet than inside a closed jar. Just it and me, face to face. Me, waiting for death. Then it crouched and I felt my hair stand on my head, like a dog's. It was like that for a while, its face close to mine, the stench of his breath just inches from my nose. I guess he was expecting I would open my eyes and look at it, but I didn't. Then it laughed. A malignant laughter that I will never forget. It sounded raspy, like dry leaves swept by the wind. Then it snorted like something that has a big chest, picked something up, stood up and left."

"I heard it go into the bush. Even then it took me several minutes which felt like an eternity to dare to open my eyes. See, I thought it might have teased me into believing he was gone and then still be there, biding its time. I feared if I opened my eyes, I would find its face two inches from mine and go insane. When the noises around me became normal again and my dogs started to shuffle and moan impatiently, I finally opened my eyes."

"It was gone, and it had taken my rabbit. Its feet had not left any traces in the snow, even though I had clearly heard the crunching of its steps at my back. I packed up and made my way home, because I knew if I stayed for the night, I would never wake up. I'll never forget that day and I hope not to ever come across the creature again."

Tom was taken aback by the story because he knew Jack very well, and he knew he was no liar. He was a leader of his community, a very reasonable man with whom he liked to sit down to discuss administrative problems with a cup of coffee. On the other hand, his dignity was natural to him. He did not need to lie to gain it. What scared that man in such a way? That man who had faced predators, freeze, famine, disease, white men, and death during his life. Did all his nightmares and fears show up together in a monumental hallucination that day in the bush? All the fears and ghosts he had not had time to entertain when he was too busy surviving? Or perhaps…? Perhaps… And that perhaps was what held the choice of accepting the magic, the unknown, the legend, as a part of our community, of the human race, as another issue in the agenda. Picasso had once said, 'Whatever can be imagined, exists.' Did the Bushman exist? Was it imagined? Did the difference matter?

There were more stories of the Nah'Gaa during that meeting, and only when the last one was done, Jimmy stood on his crutches and on his dignity, that was especially present because it was supported by his pain.

"The gravel isn't the issue today," he said. "It's not good because my people don't think it is. After all, this is the soil we step on. Our land. It's as necessary for us to bury that gravel as it is for others to build a church. Me, I have never seen the Nah'Gaa, nor I expect to, for I don't think it will be interested in showing itself to a crippled old man. Hopefully." People chuckled. "What I've seen is what the Nah'Gaa represents: Fear," he said looking at each of one of the elders gathered there. "And fear needs no gravel to walk on. It walks all over us. All over each of us. It walked over me when my granddaughter Jiewa needed me most. It walked over my son when he could not face his own ghosts and found shelter in alcohol. It walked over you elders when you thought you could disguise his behavior by wrapping it in words." An indignant murmur rose up around all the elders but Jimmy rose his palm to placate them.

"All of you are or have been mighty hunters. You can face a hungry predator without hesitation. But you are scared of what you don't know. You are scared of your own darkness. So am I." He turned to Jiewa with his hand on his chest. "Jiewa, that's why I acted as a coward when you needed my support. Because I was more scared of the darkness I didn't know than of the darkness that was already around us. Especially around you, my children. I can't undo what happened. It's part of the past and, unfortunately, part of who I am now, but I say, let's bury our fears with this gravel. Let's have a fresh start without fear. Without anyone or anything stalking our thoughts or our dreams. See what happens. I've started by replacing the image of my son descending to his tomb with the happiness and the gratitude of spending some more time with my family, if you still want this weird old wolf in a beaver coat." Tears glittered in Jiewa's eyes while Edzo stared at his own shoes.

Jimmy sat down, exhausted but at ease, as if his heavy load had been lightened. There was nothing else he needed to do or say. The elders looked down for a while, reflecting on his words in deep respectful silence.

"I will tell Leo to start shoveling the gravel tomorrow," said Tom. There was relieved applause. The women entered in the room with big casserole dishes full of caribou stew and bannock. The meeting was considered closed to begin the feast.

XIX

For two weeks, five workers shoveled fifty-three trucks of 'polluted gravel' from the roads and the baseball field. Another group dug a giant pit by the landfill to bury it, following the directions of the elders who supervised these works carefully, particularly Jimmy Whitefox.

Once they were done, there rose a smooth hill of freshly stirred dirt that, Tom joked, would be a monument to his understanding. A well deserved monument, at that, because it had not been easy to explain it to the big bosses who sat in their warm offices in Yellowknife.

Spring had settled down in Nogha Ti, where, like every year, the thaw had transformed the small net of roads into mud traps where it was almost impossible to drive unless one had a big truck. The seagulls that came every spring attracted by the fish of the lake, flew nervously, screaming in hunger because the layer of ice over the lake was still not thawed which made it impossible for them to fish. For the moment, they had to fight with the ravens for garbage and the air was a rumpus of beating wings and yells.

One afternoon, when Jimmy was smoking in his porch after supper, he listened to a real hullabaloo of birds four houses away from his, right on the big log cabin where Tom, the administrator, and his wife lived. He squinted in an attempt to figure out what was going on and saw, astonished, the foreign woman, whose pregnancy was now quite visible, throwing bread at the seagulls in front of her porch. Not some crumbs either, but what seemed to be two bags of bread gone bad. Jimmy was about to stand up and scream a warning to her, but he was too amused and his naughty boy part kept him there watching in chuckling expectation.

The woman watched how the birds gathered around the bread greedily after one week without fishing. She didn't appear to realize how alarmingly fast the community of diners was growing, making a tight tapestry of hungry birds that screamed and attacked each other fiercely for a bite of food.

When the birds started to cover her roof and her neighbor Isidore's sheets that were left outside to dry, the woman's smile faded. Her little dog, a Boston Terrier who used to play soccer with the local kids, was shielded behind her legs, aware of the fact that if he jumped at the birds, he would be devoured in seconds.

Isidore's wife opened the door briefly to see what the hullabaloo was about. She immediately shut it and stayed in. By now, the ravens had arrived too, to take part in the feast, and the space between both houses was a tight rambling battlefield of cawing, screaming, and wing beating. Tom's wife and dog receded slowly into the home, horrified. By then, Jimmy had guilty tears of laughter in his eyes.

The birds remained in their deadly rampage for some minutes until the last breadcrumb had been eaten. Then they flew away like an airborne stampede, leaving poor Isidore's sheets covered in shit.

Jimmy was still drying tears from his eyes and trying to contain laughter, sitting at his porch bench, when a voice startled him. He turned his head and saw his granddaughter Jiewa sitting on the staircase, like a prodigy rained from the sky. He looked at her in disbelief, but did not move toward her. He didn't even dare blink, lest the mirage vanished into the air and she was no longer there.

"The sled," she said, walking up the stairs and sitting on the bench beside him. The old man remained pensive, not knowing what she was talking about, or if he was supposed to ask. "The sled," she repeated. "That's what you wanted to know, didn't you? If I had any nice memory from my father." She looked at her own hands and rubbed them between her knees. "Well, he used to take Edzo and me on the dogsled, way back when we were small. Before..." she was quiet for a moment. Jimmy nodded in understanding. Yes, before. Before the mine. Before alcohol. Before their world fell apart.

"Anyway," she continued. "He whipped up the dogs and pushed us fast, fast. My mother screamed from the window, laughing, 'Ever crazyyyy!! you're gonna get killed!!' but he pushed even faster, laughing and howling like a wolf to excite the dogs even more. We were not going anywhere in particular. It was just for fun. I loved to lay on my back on the wolfskin on the bottom of the sled and watch the blue sky and the spruce go fast above my head, listen to the hissing of the skis on the snow. It was so awesome. Life seemed to be so wonderful. And I was so proud because I had the strongest, funnest dad in Nogha Ti. Then, when we came back, exhausted, with our faces frozen and red, mom gave us chocolate milk with marshmallows. That is the best memory of my childhood."

"Well, not bad for a memory," Jimmy said, thankful, lighting a cigarette with shaking hands to disguise his tears with the smoke. Jiewa nodded.

"So, Mr. Singer says we are dysfunctional," she said matter-of-factly.

"Hmm," nodded Jimmy. "That sounds like the diagnosis of an old truck. And who would that Mr. Stinger be?"

"Mr. Singer," Jiewa laughed, and it sounded like music to Jimmy's ears. "He's the counselor at the school. He says we're dysfunctional. But that's not so bad as it sounds. Just means we have to work things out."

"Aha… And who doesn't?" Jiewa shrugged and Jimmy noticed she also had tears in her eyes, although not sad tears. At least not quite. He put his arm around her and she brusquely turned to him and hugged him tightly, and he could feel her sobbing and her tears on his shoulder.

They stayed like that, unconsciously rocking back and forth in each other's arms until she pulled away and wiped her nose with her sleeve.

"Is it okay if I start at the shop on Monday?" she asked.

"Anytime. But what about the school and Mr. Stinger?"

"I will work after school," she said giggling. "Bye." She put her hands in her pockets and walked away, as Jimmy rushed back into his house calling Lisa's name.

XX

There is a tradition in the Dogrib Nation that consists of navigating the river by canoe from Nogha Ti to Behcho-Ko in the beginning of the fall; it is the same journey the Dogrib has been making for generations when they were nomads. They abandoned the lake and fishing before the freeze to go south and start the hunting season. These days, nobody makes this journey to survive. Trappers and hunters are disappearing and nobody needs to migrate anymore. However, the tradition remains an important initiation landmark in every man and woman's spiritual growth.

Every year this journey gathers elders and teens so that the youth can learn about the flowing of life and about reading the messages and warnings of nature. It is not an easy journey. It starts in the source of the river, on the border of Nogha Ti Lake, where people gather with their canoes. At three hundred metres the river falls into deep thunderous horseshoe shaped waterfalls approximately fifty metres high that, during the winter, offer a breathtaking show of massive ice blocks stopped in mid fall showing all the hues of turquoise, navy blue, and sapphire that stretch in fancy icicles under which the movement of the water can be heard, divined, and sometimes glimpsed.

During the summer this monumental obstacle must be saved by the voyagers by carrying their canoes down the slope around it. It is a steep incline covered in slippery dirt, bush, rocks, and fallen trees torn by the ice. Downhill, the stream gathers into rapids, slowing down after the waterfall jump and then soothes down to become a navigable stream.

The descent of the incline is not an easy job. The canoes are loaded with the travelers' backpacks containing food and all the necessary equipment for the three-day journey. There is not a path, so one has to advance through the tight bush, over slippery sharp stones. The heat, the bugs, and the dust surround the carriers, and there is also the occasional hungry bear attracted by the smell of the food. Once on plain land, the voyagers throw their canoes on the river and navigate the trajectory to Behcho-Ko on the safe calm river.

This would seem quite the feat, especially considering that most of the voyagers are elders, but it happens that these elders are thin, agile, hardened, and resilient little people that do not match at all a white man's image of an elder.

That summer, the elders had decided that Jiewa should make the journey in one of the canoes and the girl was not charmed with the idea. The whole family had gone to the river's edge to say goodbye. The five of them walked in silence up to the plateau where the journey would begin, at about two hundred metres from the waterfall. The whole village was gathered there. They were roasting caribou and fish in improvised barbecues and they had set up a tipi where they were celebrating a hand game. The drums and the songs joined the thunder of the waterfall.

Jimmy smiled, inhaling, delighted by the smell of the meat, the spruce fire, the fresh breeze that surrounded the river. Jiewa, however, was not enjoying any of these things. Her eyes were reddened as a result of a violent fight lost to her mother in her vain attempt to escape the journey that seemed to her tedious, useless and 'totally awful.'

After the lunch and the old songs that Jiewa barely tolerated, sitting on the floor with her arms crossed, the group walked to the upper part of the waterfall, where the incline showed itself as an impossible challenge. Jiewa looked at it, petrified. "Seriously?!" she said, her arms still tightly closed, as though to prevent her people's culture from entering her chest. Her mother, ashamed of Jiewa's attitude, was carrying the girl's backpack, for she had refused to do so after the prohibition to bring her ipod. The group moved ahead way into the incline, already lifting the canoes over their old shoulders.

Cynthia pushed Jiewa towards the group, shouting something at her in Dogrib, recriminating her for not greeting with due respect the elders that would be her journey companions, who were gathered there smoking and laughing. Cynthia refrained herself from slapping Jiewa. Mr. Singer had warned her against any kind of violence, but her palms itched to give her a good whack, and the girl's eyes glared with rage and challenge.

"Whaddya gonna do? Gonna slap me?" she shouted. "Go ahead, you bitch. Go on and slap me! If you dare!"

Her mother couldn't help raising a hand, but she lowered it and shouted, "Pick up your stuff, you little shit, don't embarrass me anymore!"

"No I won't pick up nothing!" Jiewa screamed. "Fuck you!"

The elders said nothing. They just smiled because they were about to start the journey once again and they were thankful to life for giving them one more summer and for producing this glorious fall morning, with sun beams that still warmed the bones, and for the breeze that smelled of spruce, for the waterfall music, for the laughter and songs and reminiscing that they would have during the journey.

In a moment, as though something invisible in the air had prompted them, they all put their backpacks in the canoe, including Jiewa's, put the canoe on their shoulders and walked down the incline, following the other canoes. Jiewa was literally pushed to follow them. They made their way through the bush with slow wise steps, the murmur of the people upstairs, and the music, and the drums, faded away, muffled by the trees and the waterfall's overpowering rumble. They entered the realm of magic and memories that were almost tangible in the dust suspended in the sunbeams.

Jiewa advanced behind them snorting, stomping the ground, crying in anger. It was hot. Hundreds of mosquitoes swarmed their faces and the hard branches of the bush scratched her legs mercilessly. And there she was. Stuck with a bunch of boring old farts for no less than three days. Could it get any worse? Why did those people smile, anyway? What was fun in heat, dust and mosquitoes? What was fun in old age? None of them seemed to be affected by her anger, but they kept their stupid smiles immune to her tirade of verbal and gestural violence, accepting her rage as a part of the environment, without getting involved, in the same way as they listened to the roar of the waterfall but they would never cross into its way.

Alone with five elders whose language she did not even understand. That was her family's idea of a holiday travel. She'd rather go to Edmonton, shop around, walk around the mall…Hell, her stupid mom had not even allowed her to take her iPod.

As she got more and more entangled in her thoughts, rage grew more and more present in her stomach. Alas, all she could do was obey and accompany the elders, because they had asked her in and she owed them respect. This, she knew, was a stone law in her community. The bloody journey had to be done. Hopefully, at least, there would not be so many friggin' bugs in the river, she thought as she shook them away with her hand.

And what would be on TV in this moment, she wondered. She knew the daily programming almost by heart, so she reckoned in less than an hour her favorite show would begin, where Ashton was about to tell his girlfriend that her best friend was pregnant with him. And Jiewa was going to miss the whole thing. She would have to hear the details from other people.

She liked the small group of friends in the show. They had a sweetsour taste to her, of all what she wanted in life but would never have in that fucking isolated village. Of all the beauty and the glamour she dreamed for herself, which clashed with the reality of her actual chubby uncared for body. The thing was, ever since her father started to play those games with her, those games which memory made her retch, she had taken to eating. She ate and ate and ate herself stupid while she watched TV. And she felt safe, comfortable, out of reach from life. She disguised her sexuality with pounds of flesh. Buried herself in fat to muffle the pain of her own image. So said Mr. Singer, at least.

Now that her father was dead and her grandpa's presence had grown, she was feeling safer. More accepting herself. Mr. Singer helped, too. *Stinger*, according to grandpa, she thought with a smile. Poor grandpa. He was trying really hard after screwing up with her. She liked his thick white hair, his smoker's laugh, his smell of tobacco and spruce. When he was around, problems seemed to recede, everything seemed much easier. And perhaps it was actually easier now.

The incline became steeper as they descended toward the rapids. The loose dirt was slippery and every step was an invitation to injury. And yet those elders walked weightlessly, carrying the loaded canoe with ease, as though it was made of paper, as though their aged feet were animals unattached to their bodies, seeking their way through roots, bush, and stones, as though their bones were made from a matter as light as a moonbeam.

Then one of them emitted a monotonous note as sweet as honey. "Eeeeeeeh." It was the beginning of a song, sparkling like the rapids beside them, bluish like the sky. It was a Dogrib love song. The others joined with deep serene voices in only one tone that sounded of birds and breeze. Jiewa snorted impatiently and kept walking in an outraged silence while the slithering melody impregnated the canoe, the dirt, the trees, the river, and the universe. It was a song of melancholy, of past loves, of the warmth of present loves, of poorness and hunger and socks with holes, of the flowing of all the different kinds and sizes of love. Love permeated the melody and filled the air.

Love unavoidable, dense, sweet, and all-encompassing. Jiewa felt that something inside her stretched and yawned back to life, dissolving the rage with light. Something that had remained dormant for years. Her spirit? Gradually, she uncrossed her arms to balance them rhythmically as she walked lightly over the difficult surface of the incline, as her grandparents had taught her. Her lips relaxed into something akin to a smile and her face beamed with the beauty of the transit between childhood and womanhood. A mixture of passion and melancholy.

The outside world escaped like smoke, the one that really exasperated her, the shrill sounds of her play station, the school, the skinny precious rich dolls that laughed at her from the TV shows, the obsession to leave her people and become like them, the awareness that she would never get it, the emptiness of being excluded, of having been brought up in a midland between her torn roots and her uncertain future. She sighed loudly and suddenly it was all gone. So easily.

Suddenly there was only that love song that brought her back to a place which each of her molecules remembered and identified. A place where she belonged, where her name was sacred and her life was full of stories worthy of being told by the fire. A place that smelled of spruce and caribou meat, of wild berries and fresh water, where she would never be a stranger nor feel lost. And that place was precisely around her, in the unique vibration of the bush sounds and the elders' love song. There was no hate, no pain that could banish the joy of belonging in that prodigy, of finally finding the mirror where she could see her real soul.

Slowly, almost unconsciously, her lips started to vibrate and her voice joined the elders' voices, was assimilated in the love song. She approached the group and joined it, her strong young shoulders ready to carry the canoe, which was received with smiles as sweet and beautiful as hers. Her journey had begun.

XXI

Mason Leduc was sitting in front of the impressive jacaranda bureau his mother had imported from Buenos Aires as a present for his appointment as the Bank's Vice President. "Surround yourself with good furniture," she had said, satisfied, as she supervised the installation of the massive bureau. "That way, people will understand you are here to stay. Most people will measure you by things like your car, your suit, and your office. Even by the size of your wife's boobs. Very few throughout your life will take the bother to discover your true self and those, Mason, you are not going to meet here, in this office."

As always, his mother had been right. In spite of having spent her life escaping social clichés and doing whatever she fancied, she knew the rules of the game. Or perhaps it was just because of that, because a good transgressor must necessarily know the rules she's breaking. And did she ever know them. It was as though she had read a secret manual and, after memorizing it, she had dropped it in the dustbin.

The truth was that office where he had spent a disproportionate amount of his own money, had eased his job in so many ways. Its sober solid beauty seemed to impress visitors, to put them in a mood to negotiate, in a mood to trust. Besides, with the passing years, the room had acquired his own scent, a mix of leather and unlit Cuban cigars. Mason had a very sharp sense of smell, and he believed that, when a man gave his own particular scent to an office, it meant he had conquered his position in whatever he did there. And he was, indeed, in that gratifying stage of his life.

His bureau was not covered with papers, but clean and ordered, with two or three expensive objects and his white laptop as his only tool. In front of him, a large glass wall showed Vancouver harbor, the forest of white masts of the sports vessels that separated the tall buildings from the grey immensity of the Pacific Ocean, where his gaze was now resting.

He could have gone home long ago. He was not one to spend long hours in the office. He did not need it for his accomplishments nor for his image and he liked to spend time with his family. Have dinner together and watch a movie. But he was stuck in the metallic sky of this slow autumn sunset, shuffling memories in his mind.

Behind him there were two nineteenth century maritime aquarelles chosen and paid by him, surrounded by wooden shelves loaded with Economy and Law books. In the other only wall that was not made of glass, a mahogany door opened to a silent anteroom where an effective and trustworthy secretary did half of his job for a tenth of his salary.

There were a plush leather sofa and two leather armchairs by that door, around a coffee table that matched the bureau, although not in a symmetrically perfect way and by the corner, a wooden file cabinet contained his few personal files. Behind it, a modern oil painting depicting the cathedral of Montreal under the rain hid his safe.

He took off his glasses and left them on the desk as he rubbed his eyes wearily. Mason had never considered himself a genius. Not even a very intelligent man. He was convinced that his success rested on his good organization skills and on his common sense, which of course, he had not inherited from his eccentric mother. His mother had spent her life in a parallel universe of magic and amazement that he had censored, but secretly envied, contemplating it as though through a window. Often she generously invited him to her own fantasy world and he treasured the memories of the bright colors, sweet scents, and melodious music he could only feel through her.

Mason Leduc regarded himself as a rational man whose art consisted of establishing a discipline of routines that led to a comfortable stable success. Perhaps people around him considered him dull and not aggressive enough for the present times, but they also knew he was honest and trustworthy. And he got the job done. Exceedingly well, too.

Nevertheless, he had not been himself ever since he had received that man's phone call and he could not find a way to allow himself to forget it and move on with his life. The man had been shocked beyond words by the news of his mother's death. Jimmy Whitefox was his name. The same name that was in the envelope he had been carefully saving for over two years. The envelope his mother had given him when the disease was already winning the game to her enthusiasm.

It had been during a lunch at their favourite restaurant by the harbor. She had eaten her seafood crepes without the greedy girl smile that had always made Mason look around with combined embarrassment and amusement. When they brought the coffee, she opened her purse and took out the envelope. She gave it to him so that it wouldn't get stained with food.

"What is this, mom?" he asked

"This," Veronique said arching her eyebrows and wiping her lips with the tip of her napkin, "is one of those mortifying assignments us dying entrust to those who have the precious privilege of time to carry them out. The addressee is very important, as you can imagine, and the letter, as you must have surmised by the sealing wax, is con-fi-den-tial," she said with a wink. "The contents are also very important, so I want you to deliver it personally and to make sure it is opened and read by its receiver. Not that I doubt he's going to read it." She chuckled like a schoolgirl, sipping her espresso. "This man was always crazy about me. But sometimes, old age steals our memories. And although I believe Jimmy must have held onto mine, I want to make sure that this letter brings it back."

"Jimmy Whitefox, Nogha Ti, Northwest Territories," he had read, politely astonished. "No more details?"

"It won't be necessary," she said reclining on her chair. "There must be five hundred people in Nogha Ti and they all know Jimmy."

"Would not UPS suffice?" he asked tentatively.

"Nice try, son, but no. I said deliver by hand," she said with a smug smile. "Besides, UPS does not reach Nogha Ti."

In the office, Mason shifted uneasily on his expensive leather armchair. He could never have denied this mission because that is something you just do not do to your dying mother. But for sure she had chosen quite an exotic mission, especially for a man whose time was measured to the very minute. *Where the heck was Nogha Ti, anyway?* he wondered, angrily. He googled it in his laptop, horrified.

With insecure steps, he went to the oil painting with the cathedral of Montreal and pushed the button that revealed the safe. He opened it and took the envelope out. It had been there since his mother's death, two years ago. And it would have remained there, weighing on his heart every passing day, had not been for the man's unexpected phone call. It was as if he was unknowingly claiming his letter, as if the letter had gained now a special light that crossed the safe, the painting and Mason's heart. It was his mom's last wish. But, was it fair that he became mixed in her unusual fancies? Was it fair that he had to travel to the end of the world to deliver an envelope to a person he did not even know? Who was that man, that Jimmy Whitefox? What fascination had he produced in his mother to leave him a confidential sealed letter? And last but not least, where the hell had his mom got the sealing wax?

He shook his head, smiling in spite of himself, as he returned to his desk turning the envelope in his hands. He knew the seal very well, though. It was from the ring she had sometimes hanging on a chain on her neck, since it was too big for her fine fingers. It had belonged to her grandfather and it represented some rancid noble title back in Ireland. They had buried his mom wearing that ring.

Mason was not curious about what was inside. Probably just a goodbye letter or a remembrance that was important only for two old lovers. What he felt was a certain resentment for having to carry out his mom's posthumous fancies, in which he had not part whatsoever. There you go. Northwest Territories. The ultimate frontier. As if he had nothing better to do with his time. He called his secretary and asked her to come in.

"Barbra, let's see… when do I have three or four days available?" They studied his agenda carefully and decided the following week was the most convenient.

"After that we will start with the audit and it will be quite crazy, Mason."

"Whatever you say. You're the boss," he said, not totally joking.

"So, you're finally going to take a holiday? It was about time. It's been more than a year since the last time."

"No. I'm afraid it's no holiday," he said. "Just some private business related trip… Diamonds." He improvised when he thought about the area. "I need to go to Nogha Ti, in the Northwest Territories. I don't think my wife and sons would find it exciting at all. Plus it is just a short trip. Could you get me the connections?"

"Sure!" she agreed. "As soon as you spell the name for me, please."

"Yes, but leave it for tomorrow, Barbra. There is no hurry and it's late. You should have left more than an hour ago," he said guiltily.

"No rush, boss," she said amused. "Phillip is picking me up to go for dinner at the harbor, besides I'm itching to see how to get you to this exotic place. She left the office giggling.

She came back some minutes later, bringing along a scary two page itinerary. First he had to fly to Calgary, then Edmonton, then Yellowknife and the last part he had to do with a company called *Air Tindi*. Mason put his hand over his eyes at the sight and Barbra could not contain crazy laughter any longer.

XXII

"Mason Leduc," said the man offering a brief strong handshake rehearsed in hundreds of meetings. Jimmy stood for a moment on the doorsill, striving to remember.

"We spoke on the phone," the man explained. "I'm Veronique Leduc's son".

"Ah, of course! Sorry, I went blank for a moment. Jimmy Whitefox," Jimmy answered. "Come in, please," he said guiding Mason into the living room as he looked at him up and down, trying to recognize in his person some trace of his extraordinary mother. Mason instinctively chose the dining room table instead of the comfy sofas to sit down. He felt more at ease with a table in front of him. More in his turf. Lisa served them some tea and homemade cookies and went to tend to the store. When she shut the door, she left an uncomfortable silence between the men.

"It is such an unexpected pleasure to meet you," Jimmy said, chewing his cookie. "Your mother was, and still is, one of the most important presences in my life. We were very close, you see. And even now, it is hard for me to reckon what extraordinary thing did she see in someone as plain as me," he said smiling wistfully and shrugging. "Whatever it was, I was lucky to share her magic for some time."

Jimmy supposed that the man had taken the bother to come this far for something important, not just to shake his hand, so he gave him his time.

"Pleasure's all mine," he said, clearing his throat. "You must have been very important for my mother, too. Before dying, she gave me this envelope for you." He produced it from the inside pocket of his leather jacket. "She made me promise I would deliver it personally to you, so here I am."

Jimmy took the envelope with care, as though it were a wounded bird, or a butterfly, without being able to keep his hands from shaking. He looked at it for a long moment. His name written with Veronique's terrible handwriting. A blizzard of memories shook him to the marrow, taking him by surprise.

"It's been two years," Jimmy said, raising a reproachful stare to the man.

"To be honest," Mason said, after clearing his throat again, "I have had it all this time in a safe. I knew I would have to bring it to you sooner or later, but I could never find the time. Please understand I have a very absorbing job, and a family to tend to."

"No, I don't understand," Jimmy said simply, still turning the envelope in his hands. "But that's because I'm a Dogrib and for my people, the dead's wishes are sacred."

"Anyhow," said Mason rubbing his nose uneasily. "I was instructed by my mother to stay here and make sure you read the letter. So if you don't mind, since I'm here I would like to follow my assignment to the end. I hope it won't take you long and then I can leave and take the evening flight back to Yellowknife."

Jimmy opened the envelope shaking his head in an amused disapproval.

Dear Jimmy,
The man who has just delivered this letter to you, Mason, is your

son. I know I must have left you speechless. I hope they let me get back from Heaven, or from wherever I happen to be, to see your face in this moment, because I am going to have such a laugh at your expression. Needless to say Mason does not know.

Throughout these years I have maintained the lie that he is the son of a businessman from Toronto who died in a plane crash when we were engaged. I do not know if he believes it or if he has deliberately chosen to believe it. I would have told him the truth when he was thirteen or fourteen, but look at him, Jimmy, so serious with his expensive clothing and his banker face, so helplessly lacking of humor sense. How was I going to tell him? Impossible. I leave the task to you, since you have always seemed to me a difficult person to embarrass.

I must admit I tricked you. I already knew I was pregnant when we went to Las Vegas. I planned the trip to see how would you feel out of your world, far from your ancestors' land. Then I thought, if he takes it well, I tell him. If he doesn't I'll just shut up. We'll see what happens. But you did not take it well at all. You were actually like a fish out of the water.

I do not blame you. I would have felt exactly the same terror if you had proposed me to live in Nogha Ti. Forgive me, my love. There was not a neutral ground for us.

Later on, I realized the magnitude of my dishonesty, but I got lazy. Things did not go bad with Mason. My ex died, leaving us on easy street and, apart from my job as a mom, which I did not accomplish badly at all, I had a lot of friends, a lot of partying, and the occasional lover every now and then. Although never anything like our love. Never.

Then when this filthy disease came, I thought many times about calling and telling you everything personally, but I could not let you see me like that, so skinny and wasted after my struggle for surviving. I wanted to stay in your heart beautiful and strong.

But don't think I was an ugly old fart, eh? Not at all. I stayed pretty presentable through the years thanks to a healthy life-loving nature, lots of exercise and sex, and the expertise of a couple of cosmetic surgeons.

I am attaching a picture of me when I still looked nice, so that you remember me, although I know you have never stopped remembering me, as I haven't either. Ours was a soul-to-soul love, the kind one cannot disconnect like a lamp, but it shines forever. How poetic I am getting. It must be the proximity of death.

I know you will not hate me for having hidden your son from you for all these years. Not that I do not deserve it, but you have never been able to stay angry at me for more than five minutes

Isn't he handsome? I know you are already throwing glances at him over this letter. He has become a very good looking man. He is no less than vice president of a bank in Vancouver. He has a wife and two children (our grandchildren) who are even more handsome than him. And more fun. Isn't it incredible, Jimmy, all the life we have generated even staying apart?

Please, accept him and love him. I know he is going to be shocked with the news, but then he is going to love having a father like you. He has spent all his life looking for one.

I love you, Jimmy. I never stopped loving you. Wherever it is we go, I'm going to be waiting for you with one of those hungry hugs you were always asking for.

Veronique

Mason yawned and rubbed his eyelids with his fingertips. He was pooped out. He had taken five flights to get there, the last one being an atrocious twin otter with old movie theatre seats and a pilot who flew like a madman to impress a young lady passenger whom he had invited to sit beside him in the cockpit.

He had hardly slept in almost twenty four hours and the resentment to his mom and her inconsiderate mission was growing exponentially to the aggravation he was suffering. He was smart enough to discern the wonderful unusual light his mother had poured over his childhood, and he did not reject it at all. The travels to exotic places, the picnics under the table in Vancouver's eternal raining weeks, the distorted Grimm Brothers tales she told, trying to contain her laughter at his amazement. Her eyes full of hunger for life.

Perhaps part of his frustration was due to the fact that he could not create that magic for his family. That whenever his mom came to mind, he could not help feeling boring and mediocre.

But then again, his life had not been that easy. He had an actual job. A tough one, at that. One that he should be doing right now. He reclined on the chair, looked at his wristwatch and crossed his arms, looking forward for that stupid rite to be over so that he could get back to the airport and work on his presentation for the meeting he had in a couple of days.

"You are my son," the old man in front of him said out of the blue.

"Beggya pardon?" said Mason, hardly containing his exhaustion and his anger.

"You're my son. It says it here. Read." He passed the letter to him as he looked at Veronique's picture with a dreamy expression.

Mason swiped the letter from the table. He took his reading glasses from his pocket, adjusted them, grimacing nervously. Because of his job, he was used to fast reading, but this he had to read twice before he could even react to its content, and as he did, he started to sweat like a farm animal.

He let go of the paper as if it were burning and raised his eyes to the old man's fascinated stare, trying to keep his composure. The news had taken him aback. He could not find the right words, or even the right facial expressions. However, the old man, after the initial surprise, seemed at peace with his newly found fatherhood, as he moved his gaze from Mason to his mother's picture, obviously studying the resemblance. When he turned to his mom's photo it was as intense as though she was present in the image.

"Do you have anything stronger than tea?" Mason asked.

"Second cupboard over the sink. Behind the cereals," said the old man without moving his eyes from Veronique's picture.

Mason stood up, trying to hide his rush to physically detach from this situation and gain some time to think. He found the bottle at once, but took some time to think alone, trying to put together the pieces of reality he had left.

"If you're drinking the bottle on your own in the kitchen," said the old man from the living room, "it would be a very selfish thing to do, since this is a dry community and all the booze has been paid dearly to a bootlegger. If you're expecting me to have a deadly stroke before you come back, you'll still have to wait some years. Luckily you have some groceries there."

Mason shut the cupboard and cursed between his teeth, ready to come back.

"Don't forget the glasses," added Jimmy. Mason turned on his heels and took two glasses from the sink. When he came back to his newly acquired father, he had lost all hope that this meeting would develop within the limits of normality. He was totally out of his turf, so he was not even going to try to pretend he was in control.

He took his place at the table and filled both glasses with the whisky. He left the bottle in the middle, as a silent referee, and took a big swig from his glass, which burned his throat and his stomach almost simultaneously.

"What in the name of God is this?" he asked, choking, looking at the liquid in tears. Jimmy shrugged with an apologetic smile.

"Hey, at the prices the bootleggers set, you wouldn't be expecting a Chivas, would ya?" and he took a long gulp of the beverage, with which he seemed astonishingly familiar.

The uncomfortable silence sat again between both men. A silence full of questions and common places that, by the moment, would have to remain in the backstage of their minds, from where they would pull them out slowly, like lake trouts. Jimmy looked at Mason, who had lost the serious controlling man mask, and now he did recognize himself in his eyes. And he did recognize her. Not only in the physical traces, but also in more subtle things that belonged to the soul.

"And you never knew…?" asked Mason.

"Never," said Jimmy. "And not for lack of love, gotta tell you. I loved her with all my heart. It was not just an affair. It was as she said in her letter," he said taking it carefully from the table, as though he still could not believe it existed. "It was never really over. She was the love of my life," he simply said, and he emptied his glass in a gulp. "She was the passion, the madness, the magic. She made me feel my heart was going to jump out of my chest. Made my days brighter. Much brighter…" he repeated, lost in reminiscing.

"We never spoke about the future but I think it was because we both knew it could not last for us," Jimmy continued while refilling his glass. "We belonged to different planets, like she says in her letter. There was not a middle ground for us to meet. So, even though it was painful when it ended, none of us rebelled against the end. And we should have. I don't know. It's stupid to discuss what could have been, like white men do—mind you, don't feel offended; you're not a white man anymore," Jimmy explained to Mason's wide open eyes.

"But had I known she was pregnant, I would have left everything and would have moved with her anywhere she wanted to live. Even Las Vegas. Perhaps because she knew me and knew what I would do, she never told me about you."

Jimmy considered it carefully and then shrugged with a giggle. "You know, that's one of the funny things of white women: that they are always trying to rescue us guys from ourselves and our stupidity. And I would not have wanted to be rescued, but, see? Here I am again, talking like a white man, *'If only I had, if only she had,'*" he said, laughing. "I have cavorted too much with the whites and their intoxicating books.

"Then I met Lisa, my wife, and even though—no offence intended—I love her as much as I loved your mother, it's different. It is a serene love, a love of our people. No madness but lot of understanding. Yeah. A comfortable love full of understanding. She has given me a life full of warmth and happy days."

"Did you have…?" Mason started.

"No. We never had children of our own. But we adopted one. Amorak. He died in a snowstorm during the winter."

"I'm sorry," said Mason. Jimmy nodded slowly.

"But this is another story I will tell you with more time by the fire. Because important stories must be told by the fire. Especially those that hurt, like Amorak's. Fire destroys the pain and the dirty dregs that tragedy leaves behind in the dusty corners of the heart," he said looking at Mason with a broad smile he could not help returning. "Fire is important for our Dogrib culture, which is now yours, too. The thing is, even though you never met him, Amorak was your brother and you have a niece and a nephew from him. Wait until they know they have an uncle and two cousins in Vancouver."

Mason nodded in a daze. "Well, this situation is going to require that I stay a couple more days here," he said, sighing. "If you think it's all right, Mr. Whitefox."

"Of course I think it's all right," he said, laughing loudly, "but stop calling me Mr. Whitefox, for Pete's sake. I'm your father. You may start by calling me Jimmy, since judging for what I know about white men, it will take you some months to be able to say father. And it's okay, but don't blame me for calling you son. Can't help it. I'm an Indian and for us a son is a son, even though we have not heard of him in forty years. I'm yours already," Jimmy said.

That night, as Jimmy cuddled in bed with Lisa, who was too interested in the story to sew, he kept repeating the parts of his conversation with Mason, and how the facts had developed.

"And you, dirty old man! Coming up with extra-marital sons at this age! Be ashamed!" she said, elbowing him and laughing. "He seems a little bit smug," she whispered, as though she was scared he could hear her from the guest room.

"Well, like most white men, he somehow acts his life rather than living it. But he's a good guy. He must be, with such an awesome father." They both laughed and cuddled up closer under the duvet.

"And when will we meet the grandchildren?" she asked nervously. "I better start to make jackets and mitts for them right away. And mukluks. Ask him for their shoe sizes."

"He says we could go in Christmas. Not all of us. Just you and me. You know white men prefer to accept reality in small doses, as though that were possible."

"Hmm… that gives me time enough to make moccasins for all of them," she said, mentally calculating. "Vancouver," she added dreamily. "Never been there. There must be casinos like castles. But I don't like to leave the kids behind."

"I say we take Jiewa and Edzo. They're not going to kick them out unless they really screw up. Whites are very polite."

She giggled and turned around in bed to enjoy her excitement on her own, to relish the new dream in its full extent.

"Isn't it funny?" Jimmy said, spooning with her. "One thinks the end has come and suddenly a new beginning shows up."

Inuvik, 3rd December 2011

ACKNOWLEDGEMENTS

A huge thank you to my Publisher Halli Villegas for her trust and for the brilliant editing she did jointly with Sephera Giron. Thank you both. It is such a privilege to be edited by two remarkable writers. A special thank you to my childhood friend Javier Fruns, who edited the original Spanish version of "Lobo con Abrigo de Castor"—another privilege—and to his sister, my Friend Maria Luisa Fruns, my sister and Life Coach Beatriz Lloret and my aunt Enri Lloret, a delightfully slanted critic. I love you guys and I miss you something bad.

Last but not least, thank you Tom Matus, my husband, who guided me through the amazing North and provided me with vital information for this book. Thank you for your enthusiasm and your patience.

Canadian-Spanish author Rosario Lloret was born in Madrid, Spain. She moved to Canada in 2003 and lived in the Northwest Territories for six years. She currently resides in Hudson's Hope, British Columbia, with her husband and three daughters. *Wolf in a Beaver Coat* is her first novel.